MAMA'S

Babies

MAMA'S
Babies

GARY CREW

ANNICK PRESS LTD.
TORONTO • NEW YORK • VANCOUVER

For Nana Audrey

© 2002 Gary Crew

Annick Press Ltd.

Cover design by Irvin Cheung/iCheung Design
Cover illustration by Danuta K. Frydrych.
First published in Australia by Thomas C. Lothian Pty Ltd.

Cataloging in Publication Data
Crew, Gary, 1947-
        Mama's babies
North American ed.
ISBN 1-55037-725-6 (bound).—ISBN 1-55037-724-8 (pbk.)
        I. Title.
PZ7.C867Ma 2002   j823   C2001-903091-6

Distributed in Canada by: Published in the U.S.A. by
Firefly Books Ltd.   Annick Press (U.S.) Ltd.
3680 Victoria Park Avenue   Distributed in the U.S.A. by:
Willowdale, ON   Firefly Books (U.S.) Inc.
M2H 3K1   P.O. Box 1338, Ellicott Station
                                   Buffalo, NY 14205

Printed and bound in Canada.

visit us at: **www.annickpress.com**

PROLOGUE

At the time this story takes place, over a hundred years ago, modern methods of preventing pregnancy were unknown. It may be hard to imagine now, but back then great shame was attached to any unmarried girl or woman who had a baby. The mother not only suffered the rumor and innuendo, but also bore the responsibility of raising her child alone. The practice of baby farming emerged in this environment of fear and shame.

Many unwed mothers were teenagers, and although they often wanted to keep their babies, personal or financial circumstances frequently made this impossible. These girls were therefore forced—if only for a while—to place their babies in the hands of another caregiver. Some young mothers advertised in newspapers for a suitable person to look after their child. These brief and heart-wrenching ads sought the aid of women who loved children and who, for a small payment each week, would care for a baby until the unfortunate mother could reclaim it and raise it herself. There is little doubt that most young mothers hoped this period of separation would last only a few weeks at most.

While many of the women who answered

these ads were trustworthy, some were not. Certain "baby farmers" (the term that came to be used for women who provided full-time child care) were unscrupulous, often supplying false references or personal qualifications, or lying about their circumstances in order to obtain the money offered by the desperate mother. They might reply to an advertisement in this manner: "Bereaved mother of recently deceased child, would dearly love a baby of her own..."

Eager to have her child cared for, the young mother would readily accept—if she could afford the fee. Next, the baby farmer would arrange to meet the mother and take the baby. Railway stations were always considered convenient venues because of their bustle and the anonymity they afforded. Here the mother would hand over her child, complete with favorite toys, soft blankets, and sometimes extra money for a Christmas or birthday present.

Sadly, some of these babies did not live long. Wanting only the cash premium paid by the unsuspecting young mother for the first few weeks of care, a cold-hearted baby farmer might murder the child, then dispose of the body, thus clearing the way for another child (and another cash payment).

Another hateful part of this practice was that unethical baby farmers sometimes "adopted" girls from welfare or charitable institutions to care for the infants. These girls then became virtual slaves to their adoptive "mama." They knew that if they complained about their conditions, they would be sent back. Applying emotional blackmail, the baby farmers had these girls do the heavy chores about the house until the "mama" disposed of the infants left in her care.

Baby farming was practiced all over the Western world. Eventually, some women were convicted of the murder of as many as fifteen babies. This criminal scheme was not stopped until social workers, charitable institutions, police, and newspaper owners combined forces to prevent such women from preying on more innocent young mothers.

This novel is based upon the murderous careers of three baby farmers of the 1890s: Amelia Dyer (London, England), Minnie Dean (Winton, New Zealand), and Frances Knorr (Melbourne, Australia). All were sentenced to death as a result of the testimony of teenage girls who had been employed by them.

Gary Crew
Queensland, Australia
October 2001

Advertisement in the *Sydney Tribune*,
March 5, 1894:

WANTED: Caring mother to adopt infant aged 15 months. Premium of ten pounds will be paid to suitable applicant. Contact "Mother," Post Office, Hurstville.

1
A PARCEL
CHANGES HANDS

By the time I was nine years old I had begun to doubt that Mama Pratchett, the woman with whom I had lived for as long as I could remember, was in fact my mother. My doubts were based upon a growing understanding that no woman, not even Mama Pratchett, could possibly have given birth to five further children aged at that time between one year and five, especially since none were twins. Yet there we were, living under one roof, all six of us calling her "Mama."

With so many little ones about, it also seemed strange that there was no "Papa Pratchett," and question Mama as I might, I was unable to establish that there ever had been.

There were more sinister reasons for my doubts. While all of Mama's children, from babes in arms to toddlers, seemed simply to appear, there were others who disappeared just as suddenly, often before I had even learned their names.

It was sudden appearances and disappearances, more than any other circumstance, that led me, at last, to suspect Mama Pratchett. And to observe her ways.

"Sarah," Mama said to me one morning, "I want you to come down to the station with me. Leave the children. We won't be long."

That Mama was going "down to the station" was not at all unusual. In fact, railways in general seemed to be a part of her reason for being. No matter how often we shifted house (which was very often, and for no good reason that I could detect), our new abode was always beside the line, often a former railway worker's shack, now cheaply rented, or once, when we were very lucky, a little stone cottage that had been the station master's. But the strange thing about Mama's going this morning was that I had been invited, a circumstance which had never occurred before. For this reason alone I was eager to oblige.

"When?" I asked, giving a firm wring to the diapers I was washing.

"I'm due to meet the ten-fifteen from Peachester," she said. "I have a parcel to collect. I mustn't be late."

"A parcel?" I queried. "If it's only a bundle of sewing, couldn't it be left with the station master? I could collect it when I have finished here."

Mama made what little money came into our house by working at home as a seamstress. It was quite common for her customers to send her bundles of clothes by rail. But in this case it seemed that my assumption was wrong.

"No," she declared in a tone that would brook no argument, so I left the diapers to soak, pulled on my bonnet, and waited dutifully by the gate with a swarm of little ones hanging on my skirt and begging to come with me.

Mama appeared soon after, decked out in her best to meet the train. Perched upon her steely gray hair, which she parted in the center and pulled back into a bun, she wore a pillbox hat of black satin, tied beneath her many chins with a most audacious bow. Mama was a naturally imposing woman, big-boned and heavy-set, but when these physical attributes were accentuated by her particular choice of clothing, especially severely cut skirts and jackets (usually of battleship gray), her black stockings, walking shoes, and an enormous black leather handbag, she was truly a force to be reckoned with.

"Hurry up," she called as she reached the gate, and when I had disengaged myself from the children, I followed hastily, feeling a little like a dinghy dragged in the wake of a mighty vessel.

To be addressed gruffly was not new to me. Being the eldest of the children and the one who had been with Mama the longest, it had fallen to my lot to be treated more as a maid than as a daughter — except that a servant would have been paid and a daughter would have been loved. I had never been fortunate enough to receive either love or money. In those days I believed that this lack of attention or affection was due to my being plain. It is true that I was pale and thin, my face pinched, my eyes gray, and my hair mousy and lank. Nor did I have a vivacious or winning personality. Still, since it was pointed out to me daily that I was lucky to have a roof over my head and food in my stomach, I did not complain.

So I hurried along behind Mama, thankful for the opportunity of breaking the monotony of my day and excited at the thought of seeing Mama's mysterious parcel, particularly as it was too important — or possibly too precious — to leave in the care of the station master.

At that time we were living on the outskirts

of a village called Waterford. It was a miserable place. Once, they said, it had thrived on the extraction of peat from the swampy, wind-driven wasteland that surrounded it, but when the peat proved to be of too poor a quality to extract, the industry had failed and the population moved away. Now the village was almost deserted. One or two old folk remained, including the grocer, Mr. Dibbs, who sold little more than moldy potatoes. And there was the railway station, manned solely by the station master, Mr. Quaver. He was aptly named considering that, through either age or some terrible affliction, he spoke in a curious high-pitched tremolo, rendering most of what he said — which was not much, since he was a solitary individual — very difficult to understand.

Yet everything about Waterford was not as gloomy as the picture that I have painted. There was one salvation. This was the nephew of the wretched Mr. Quaver, a boy called Will who would often take the train from Ipswich, where he lived and went to school, to spend the weekend with his lonely uncle or, more correctly, to wander among the reedy pools and dense thickets of the swamp in search of adventure.

I first met Will Quaver when he passed our

shack one day. Hearing my charges squealing in the front yard, I left my sweeping and went to the door to look. In the middle of the road was a gangly red-headed boy, perhaps a year or two older than myself, entertaining the children by performing cartwheels and handstands. I saw the boy as no more than a show-off and would have shooed him away with my broom if he had not caught sight of me and ceased his display immediately.

"Hello there," he said. "I'm Will Quaver. My Uncle Bertie's the station master." His manner was so pleasant that I could even forgive him his shock of hair, which appeared to have been struck by lightning. "Are all of these kids your brothers and sisters?"

As amiable as he seemed, the boy was still a stranger and, as such, a threat that Mama would never tolerate — particularly a stranger who asked questions about her children. Once, when I had plucked up the courage to ask her why other children couldn't visit, she turned upon me and said, "What? Aren't there enough already?" Which was true, I suppose.

And so, when Will Quaver asked about the children, reasonable as his question was, I replied, "That is none of your business. Now be off with you," adding, as Mama would have done, "Children, come inside this minute." The pity was that I was not Mama, and neither the boy nor the children moved. "Do you hear me?" I bawled again, at which Will Quaver laughed.

"Well, well," he said, "it seems that you have no control over your little family. And you have none over me either, since I am on a public road."

At this I turned on my heel to fetch Mama, but by the time she had reached the door, the boy was gone, though the children still hung over the gate, calling after him as he skipped cheekily down the road.

That was my first meeting with Will, and in the three or four that followed, little advance was made, except that his persistence became more evident and my amusement at his antics and devil-may-care boldness increased. Finally, on a day when Mama had gone to the Saturday market in a neighboring town, I discovered Will in our front yard playing leapfrog with the children, and from that day on, whenever he was visiting and Mama was away, he would come to play.

On this particular morning, as I trooped silently to the station in Mama's ample wake, I noticed that Will was sitting on the edge of the platform, his skinny legs dangling so far over the side that the soles of his boots almost touched the shiny rails below. On seeing him there, I felt a sudden flush rise from my neck to my cheeks. What if he saw me and called to me? Worse, what if he asked after the children? How would I explain our acquaintance to the ever vigilant Mama? And how she would box my ears for allowing a stranger to befriend our little band.

So I averted my eyes, lowered my head, and pulled down my bonnet in readiness for the moment when Mama and I must step up onto the platform. I thought that I would faint when, quite suddenly, Mr. Quaver's peculiar bird-like voice called from the ticket box, "Mrs. Pratchett, Mrs. Pratchett, do wait, please." Before he could reach us, I saw Will approaching.

"Might I help you, Ma'am?" he asked in a most gentlemanly way and, doffing his cap, he offered his hand to Mama.

Now I cannot be sure that such a courtesy had ever been so nicely presented to her before, and for an instant she fairly stopped mid-stride, then she raised her hand as elegantly as you like, saying, "Why, thank you, young man. You know a hard-working woman when you see one." At this, Will hauled her onto the platform while I stepped up briskly behind.

While Mama rearranged her bonnet, Will

gave me a quick wink, then slipped from sight behind the ticket box, leaving me to reflect that, while he might be a "stranger" by Mama's terms, to me he was a friend.

At precisely ten-fifteen by the station clock the Peachester train arrived. For the life of me I had no idea why the station existed, considering so few people used it, except for Mama's regular trips and, at odd weekends, Will Quaver — and he traveled free anyway, since his Uncle Bertie was in the railway. The train stopped amidst a gush and a hiss of steam and a belch of thick black smoke. This was accompanied by a great deal of flag-waving and whistle-blowing by Uncle Bertie, who, I think, was doing his best to look important.

Of course the real importance of the arrival for me was the mysterious parcel, and I watched the guard's van expectantly for him to emerge with a box or bundle. But activity at the far end of the train was limited to a disembodied hand waving a green flag, and I had begun to doubt that anything was to arrive at all when Mama suddenly rushed up to a carriage and yanked a door open. Then, to my utter astonishment, there appeared first one, and then another, suitcase and, following these, a very pretty young woman, dressed in the smartest of city clothes, an ostrich feather sweeping grandly from her hat. It was to this woman that Mama presented herself — with the hint of a curtsey, I thought. Before I could recover from my surprise, what appeared to be a bundle of clothes was handed to her, followed immediately by a long white envelope which Mama dropped into her handbag, clicking it firmly shut. At this the young woman returned to her carriage and closed the door. The whistle sounded, a hand with a red flag waved from the guard's van, there was a further gush and hiss of steam, the belch of thick black smoke was repeated, and the train pulled out, the pretty young woman sitting hunched at her carriage window with a white lace handkerchief covering her face.

I did not know what to think, and was about to express my confusion when Mama barked, "Well, Missy, pick up the cases. That's what you were brought for." I had just bent to do as I was told when a familiar sound from the bundle in Mama's arms made me straighten up. The "parcel" that she had been so eager to receive was a baby!

2

AN APPEARANCE
AND A
DISAPPEARANCE

Although my mind was fairly bursting with
questions, I had little opportunity to put them to
Mama, saddled as I was with the two suitcases,
which I was obliged to carry all the way home.
Mama, on the other hand, strode on ahead, the
baby cradled in her arms. By the time I reached
the house she was already seated in the kitchen,
giving it a bottle, while the little ones crowded
around her, all clamoring for a look.

"What shall I do with the cases?" I asked,
setting them down in the hall, which was the
only place there was a square inch of room left
among the mattresses, cribs, and cots that were
all about.

"Well, you can't leave them there," she

answered curtly. "Put them on my bed until I can attend to them."

Mama slept in a single bed in the tiny front room. It was the only place in the house where the children were not allowed, and where even I rarely went, except on Mama's orders. Not that I minded. The room was so filled with piles of clothes and shoes and blankets and caps and bonnets that it looked more like a stall at a rummage sale than a bedroom. And when Mama herself was sleeping there, her mountain of a body tossing and turning, and with her snoring and making Heaven knows what other noises beneath the covers, it was even less pleasant.

Nevertheless, as I had been told, I dragged the cases into the room and heaved them onto the bed. As I did, I caught sight of her black handbag sitting on the upturned fruit box which she used as a dressing table. The corner of the envelope which the young woman had given her at the station protruded from its clasp.

By nature I was not a deceitful child, but by this time I was sufficiently interested in Mama's ways to take any opportunity to learn more of the curious comings and goings in our house. Here, I reasoned, was such a chance, and before she could finish feeding the child or notice my absence, I unclasped the bag and removed the envelope. It was perfectly plain, bearing no address, but it had already been opened, presumably by Mama herself. This was fortunate for me, and I peered inside. To my amazement, it contained a crisp green banknote.

Having only an elementary understanding of numeracy and literacy, since Mama usually kept me from attending school (even in towns that were big enough to have one), I was still able to recognize a twenty-pound note when I saw it. Why would anyone give such a huge amount of money to Mama and, what's more, deliver it with a baby?

It was from this incident that the first intimations of Mama's real occupation crossed my mind, and with trembling fingers and a beating heart I returned the envelope to her bag, which I placed back on the box as I had found it.

Hardly had I done this than Mama yelled from the kitchen, "Are you going to feed these kids, or do I have to do that too?" which was a question — no, an order — directed at me, and I hurried out to prepare some bread and butter.

The baby was a girl and Mama told us that she was named Victoria, after our Queen. She was the dearest little thing, and no trouble, but she took up much of Mama's time, which, of course, only added to my duties. Still, I knew not to complain. Besides, Mama was always happiest with a new baby in the house, and that kept her from finding fault with me.

But the call of the railway soon struck again, and one Saturday morning she announced that she was going to market. I could not have been more pleased. This meant that I would have the house to myself and there was every chance that Will Quaver would come. I had yet to thank him for not betraying my trust the day Victoria arrived.

Sure enough, Mama's train had only just left when Will came down the road, whistling and hallooing to announce his presence. The children went wild with delight and he entertained them for half an hour before stepping up to our porch and calling, "Sarah, are you coming out?"

I was in the middle of feeding Victoria but, since Will's visit was something of a red-letter day, I brought her out and sat on the top step.

"Well," he said, "this one's new, eh?"

"She came on the train the other day," I answered, "the last time you were here."

"What, she caught the train all by herself, did she?"

"No, a very nice young woman brought her down," I replied, seeing no reason to lie, "and Mama is minding her." I was satisfied with this answer, and hoped that he would be too.

Perhaps he was, perhaps not, but he gave a dismissive sniff all the same, and asked, "So I guess that means you're minding her today?"

"Well, I don't know who else would," I said. Then, seeing him frown, I added, "Why?"

"Nothing." He moved away a little and stuck his thumbs into the pockets of his trousers. "'Cept I was wondering if you'd like to come for a walk with me down by the swamp. There's plenty of wildflowers out at this time of year ..." But here he trailed off and looked away sheepishly.

I was so taken aback that I let the bottle slip from the baby's mouth. "I'm sorry, Will, but I can't, not with the new baby. Besides, little Robbie's not twelve months yet and I couldn't leave him. And with Mama being so strict, I don't think I'd be allowed to go even if she was here. But thanks all the same. And thanks for not letting on that you knew me at the station, too. Mama would have been fit to spit if she thought I'd been talking to strangers, you know."

He gave me a quizzical look. "Well, it's about time somebody told her that I'm not a stranger.

My uncle's the station master here, so I prob'ly know more about the place than she does!"

"I'm sure you do," I agreed, "but she's funny that way. She just likes to keep the family close, that's all."

At this his face lit up. "Aha, so these kids are your family, hey? Geez, you're lucky. Me, I've got nobody, no brothers or sisters, only my mother and father, and they're no fun. That's why I come down here whenever I can. To get out, like, and have a bit of an adventure."

When Will spoke like this, it seemed that his scruffy hair stood up all the more, as if there was really electricity flowing through it. But that day there was very little I could do to help him, so I asked if he would sit beside me and tell me about the swamp, since it seemed unlikely that I'd ever have the chance to go.

Mama came home on the six-fifteen train and I had never been so glad to see her. The children were hungry and I had nothing to feed them. She went straight into her room, to change into her house clothes, I imagined, but when she reappeared she was wearing a new coat and skirt.

"A mother needs to pamper herself sometimes," she declared, looking at her reflection in the piece of mirror that was mounted behind the kitchen door. "And this mother always feels better for it." The clothes were dull gray and undersized. Personally, I thought she looked like a giant armadillo. When no one offered a complimentary word, she put her hands on her hips and puffed herself up in a truly frightening way, shouting, "Well? Well? What are you so down in the mouth about? Answer me, Miss!"

Of course "Miss" was none other than myself, always the scapegoat of Mama's tempers. Usually I yielded to her to keep the peace, but on this occasion I would not. I assumed that the money for the new clothes had come from the young woman who handed Vicky over on the railway platform, but I was equally certain that it had not been her intention to have it spent on Mama's vanity while the baby sucked at its fingers for lack of food.

"Mama," I said, "the children have had no supper. There's no milk for the baby or for little Robbie. We are all too hungry to be admiring your new clothes."

She had raised her hand to strike me as soon as I opened my mouth, but at the mention of the new baby her eyes darted to its crib. "As if I would forget the baby," she protested. "I bought her milk powder and rusks. And fat pork sausages for the rest of you. I hoped, for once, you would allow me a little pleasure. But, Miss Sarah, you were always a selfish girl, and I dare say the others have taken their lead from you. Why, without me none of you would have a roof over your head or a crust in your stomach ..." Still ranting, she went to her bedroom to return presently with the necessities for our supper.

The next morning I was not surprised to see Mama digging in the overgrown vegetable garden at the back of the house. She had a habit of gardening after one of her fits of temper. I supposed that it was a means of relaxation and I was always happy to see her so engaged. On this occasion I was even more heartened to see that she had several packets of seeds, a sign that we would be staying in Waterford long enough to see them grow.

I had just hung out the washing and was about to go in when a familiar voice called from the side of our house, "Morning, Mrs. Pratchett. What's that you're planting?"

It was not often that anything surprised Mama, but that morning Will caught her completely unawares. She straightened and turned to see who had been insolent enough to address her in such a bright and breezy tone.

"How do you know my name?" she demanded, squinting into the morning sun.

"I'm William Quaver," he answered. "My Uncle Bertie told me who you were 'cause he's the station master here. And you know," he added cheekily, "I reckon that he's got a bit of an eye for you."

Mama released an indignant "Harumph!" and, shading her eyes, gave Will a long, suspicious stare. "You're the boy from the station, eh? And Quaver's your uncle, eh?" But I could tell from her tone that she took what he had said about old Mr. Quaver as something of a compliment, and maybe Will did too, since he immediately climbed the fence and landed, light as a cat, amongst the long grass and weeds in our yard.

"And who's this?" he asked, turning to me and sneaking one of his knowing winks.

"That's Sarah," Mama said, and for some curious reason I was suddenly aware that she had never once referred to me as "my daughter," as any other mother would.

"You can call me Will." He tipped his cap, then turned again to Mama. "I can give you a hand if you want," he said. "I like having a bit of a dig. I don't mind getting my hands dirty." And he reached for the garden fork.

The change that came over Mama was as swift as it was menacing. She snatched the fork away from him as if he had attempted to steal the crown jewels. "No!" she blurted. "I don't need any help!"

Will was utterly nonplused, but I could have told him that Mama was almost fanatical about her garden. Nobody was ever allowed to play near it, and if any of the children were caught digging there, even with the best of intentions, the result was a strapping which was not a pretty sight to see.

Still, Will was quick to regain his composure. "Well then," he said with a shrug, "since I was on my way to the swamp, would you like me to take a couple of the kids for a bit of a walk? Get 'em out from under your feet, like?"

I'm not sure what came over me, but before I could stop myself I had leapt forward, crying, "Oh, Mama, let us go. I've finished the washing and I'd look after them, truly. Ben and Maggie would be no trouble. Nor would Josephine."

Mama looked at me as if she thought I had lost my mind. "And who would be minding the others while you were out there, eh?"

I was too quick for her. "Then I'll take them all. We could carry Horace and little Robbie, if I could just leave Vicky's crib down here in the shade."

Mama scowled, but I could see that she was considering. "All right," she finally muttered, "but not Robbie. I think he's coming down with something. He seems sweaty and feverish."

This sudden concern came as a surprise to me. The child had been perfectly healthy the day before, bearing his hunger like a Spartan, but Mama's opinion was never to be questioned. Besides, I had my own interests to think of, so I readily agreed to leave him. "Thank you, Mama. Thank you," I cried. "We won't be long. No more than an hour, I promise."

Then, to my further astonishment, she said, "No need to hurry. Make a day of it if you like," and so saying, she resumed her digging.

As for myself and the little ones, we had led Will out of the gate before she could change her mind.

I often stopped my sweeping to stare out over the veranda rail towards the distant swamp. Although I had never been there, the children and I sometimes walked beside it along the track that led in front of our house. In the early morning, mists rose and coiled from its hidden pits and pools, while in the evenings a fine gray smoke drifted from the heated peat that lay beneath its surface. Yet, though the swamp was dense with shrubs and reeds, we never heard the song of a bird, and the place appeared mournful and strangely joyless. It seemed to be forbidden territory, not just to us as Mama Pratchett's children, but to our feathered friends as well. Of course, all of this changed with the presence of Will and the whistles and whoops of the excited children.

Ben and Maggie, who were four and five respectively, marched on ahead, while Josephine, aged a little over three, took hold of Will's hand and held it tight. To her, this was a great adventure but, as such, bore with it the possibility of quicksand or pythons and all sorts of other exotic horrors she had heard of from our well-thumbed collection of dilapidated penny dreadfuls. As for Horace, who at two and a half was the youngest, he sat high on Will's shoulders, which gave the whole expedition the appearance of an Indian nabob's tiger hunt!

The morning was clear and hot, and as Will helped us over the stile that led to the swamp, I was already sweating. Mercifully, Horace was happy to walk — on condition that I held his hand — and I am sure that Will was glad to set him down upon the lush grass.

"Do hippypotmus live there?" he asked, his

eyes wide with expectation of the wonders that lay beyond.

Will laughed. "No, Horrie. Nothing as big as that. But we could see a turtle."

"And will it bite me?" the child asked. "Might it pull me in the water and drown me dead?"

Will laughed again. "No. It won't drown you. But if we can find a nice fat earthworm, he would eat that. That's what he would really like to eat."

On hearing this, Horace was silent and for some time directed his attention to every likely hole in the boggy ground.

No pen could possibly describe the sheer pleasure that the children derived from that morning's rambling with Will Quaver. Not only did the extent and variety of sensations provided by the swamplands exceed their expectations, but Will himself proved to be as knowledgeable of the workings of a child's mind as he was of the swamp itself. Beneath every leaf he could reveal a beetle, beneath every stone a toad, in every pool a festoon of frog's eggs. Once, to our horror, we saw the side-winding track of an enormous eel, where it had emerged from its reedy pool to slither overland in search of another.

As for my own reactions, I could not account

for the peculiar effect that the landscape had upon me. Or perhaps it was not the landscape itself, with its deep green vegetation and haunting waters, but the freedom to rove through it that so excited me. If I could, I would have dropped to my knees and gathered all that I saw in my arms, taking it back with me to our dismal house where, given a month of Sundays, I might have been better able to fill my senses with the touch, the scent, the visual pleasures which every element of that marvelous place had to offer. Dreamer that I was, I had to be satisfied with the reality of gathering sprigs of each strange and wonderful flower that I happened upon, with the intention of pressing them all as souvenirs of this wonderful day.

It was well into afternoon by the time we returned to the cottage, and the children were very tired. I said goodbye to Will at our gate, and thanked him profusely, then ushered my charges in with many warnings to be quiet, since I fully expected Mama to be deep in her afternoon nap — and we all knew better than to wake her!

To our surprise the house was empty, and the yard too, though it was evident that considerable clearing and planting had been done in the garden during our absence.

I returned to the gate and looked towards the station and the little cluster of buildings beyond. Mama was nowhere to be seen, which was most disconcerting. I had never known her to leave the house with even one baby, let alone two — yet there was no sign of either Vicky or little Robbie, and if Mama had taken him, her hands would certainly have been full!

But the needs of the hungry and overtired children were my immediate concern. Fortunately, there were a few sausages left from the night before and, with the addition of some black bread and a little dripping, I was able to prepare a filling meal, washed down with water. Having tended to this, I convinced the children to rest, and presently each was contentedly sleeping.

I admit to being concerned about the absence of Mama and the two babies but, since there was little that I could do to locate them, I set myself the task of pressing the flowers that I had brought from the swamp.

Perhaps this was the first occasion that I had reason to be thankful for one of Mama's odd habits: every Sunday she would walk to the station to collect her "Special Delivery" newspapers. Mama read every sensational article that these papers contained as if her life depended upon it. There was never an account of a society scandal, a hideous murder, or violent kidnaping that she overlooked and, what was worse, it was her delight to tell us (young Horace and Josephine included) every frightful detail over supper at night. Sometimes I would reflect what a terrible thing it was that while other families would be reading from the Scriptures, ours was subjected to the devil's own tales!

Still, on that day, I was very grateful for Mama's interest in the Sunday papers. Beside her bed was a stack of them (which regularly played host to a family of mice) and from these I gathered a bundle which I spread flat upon the kitchen table. I then sorted my blooms according to the species that Will had identified for me and placed them carefully between the pages. I was just about to fetch two broken panes of glass that had been lying in the yard, intending to press my flowers between them, when I heard Mama's unmistakably heavy tread upon the front veranda. I abandoned my attempt to play the botanist and ran out to greet her.

"Mama," I cried, "where have you been?" But before she had the chance to answer, I could already see that little Robbie was not with her. She held Vicky in her arms, and her handbag dangled from her elbow. That was all. "Where is Robbie?" I asked.

Mama said nothing but bustled through to the kitchen, where she carelessly tossed her handbag directly onto my specimens, which scattered upon the floor. Only then did she say, "It's been a long day and Mama's tired. Put Victoria in her crib and make me a nice cup of tea, then I'll answer your questions. There's a good Missy."

I hurried to comply, all the while aware that I was crushing my flowers beneath my feet.

When our chipped brown china teapot sat hot and beckoning before Mama, she poured herself a cup, added three teaspoons of sugar (which was her usual habit), took a long sip, then sat back with a satisfied sigh. "Ah, Missy," she said, "I have bad news for you. Very bad news."

At this my blood chilled. I had long ago learned what the expression "bad news" meant in the Pratchett household: one of our little ones had fallen ill. Usually so ill that we would never see him or her again. "Robbie?" I asked, pulling out a chair and sitting at the table beside Mama.

She sipped her tea before answering, although I noticed that she held her cup with both hands, possibly in an attempt to stem their evident trembling. "A turn for the worse, I'm afraid. A very bad turn."

This was information that I could barely comprehend. "But Mama," I protested, "he was so well on Saturday. He showed no sign of a fever. How could it come on so quickly?"

"When you are my age," she mused, staring down into the depths of her teacup, "and have had the experience with little ones that I have, you will know that a fever can come on in a matter of hours."

"And this happened while I was away?"

Mama nodded, slowly and methodically pouring herself another cup. "I am afraid so, Missy. Why, it was exactly as I predicted when you asked to take him. You had hardly left when I heard him crying in his cot. It was a cry that only a mother can know, I'm afraid, and I hurried to pick him up. Oh, he was hot. His dear little face and his chest, red and burning. Of course I did all I could. I bathed him in cool water to try to bring his temperature down, but that did little good, poor mite, and when I saw that look in his eyes ..."

"What look, Mama?"

"Ah, Missy, it is a look that you would never wish to see. A faraway look. As if the little one can already see into Heaven. See sweet Jesus there, waiting ..."

"No, Mama," I cried, covering my own burning ears. "That could never be so. Not with our little Robbie. Not so soon!"

"What?" she exclaimed, turning accusingly to face me. "Are you saying that our little lamb is not good enough to fly to the arms of his Saviour? Take care, Missy, that the same will not be said of you!"

"No, no, Mama, that is not what I meant at all. Quite the opposite. I meant, why would Jesus want our little boy at all? Who has he ever harmed to be taken from us? He has brought only joy. Where is he, Mama? Surely not ...?" But I could not ask the question that had formed in my heart.

"Our Robbie is in Peachester," Mama assured me. "He is with the doctor there. When I saw that he was taken so bad, I gathered up his things, and took Victoria, and hurried to catch the eleven-fifteen. The doctor thinks he may have the meningitis. The brain fever. That is a serious thing. But Missy, I don't want you to go getting and distracting yourself from your duties to the others. I have done my best for him and now he is in the hands of his Maker, and the doctor, of course ..."

For some reason, this latter assurance had a doubtful ring about it, and I confess that I continued to fear the worst.

Mama's attitude and actions over the next few days did little to make me feel any better. Instead of hurrying off daily to check on Robbie's condition, she stayed about the house, seemingly unconcerned as she tended her new garden, sewed a little, or simply sat in the sun rereading her precious papers.

It was not until the following Thursday that she finally roused herself, partly as a result of my persistent inquiries, and took the train to Peachester.

That day was one of the longest in my life, and come six o'clock I was leaning over the fence waiting for her arrival upon what I knew to be the last train. Only then did I see her making her way home from the station, her handbag swinging in her hand, apparently ignorant of the fears of those who waited for her news.

She was so slow in coming that I finally ran out to meet her on the road, calling, "Mama! Mama!" Upon hearing my voice and seeing me running towards her, she immediately increased her pace, and though the light was fading, I was certain that her expression suddenly changed from that of blissful carelessness to one of deep concern.

"Oh, Missy, Missy," she began, reaching out to gather me to her, "he is gone. Our little Robbie is dead." Then she set me down to pull her handkerchief from her handbag and made a great scene of dabbing her eyes and blowing her nose.

As for myself, I walked back beside her, neither asking for more details nor receiving any.

The following Saturday Mama returned to Peachester to attend what she termed a "private funeral" for little Robbie. I found it strange that she should set out in a suit of bright red linen, without so much as a black arm band or veil over her bonnet, but I said nothing, assuming that she must be attending to some of her sewing business later — although even that showed a lack of good taste, let alone of bereavement.

Of course, I was obliged to stay at home with the children, which was a great disappointment to me and, I know, to the older ones who had loved Robbie as much as I. Still Mama would not be swayed, no matter how much we pleaded, although when Will came to see us later, the house took on a merrier mood.

When he had played with the children, he sat with me on the veranda and asked what had happened, and why I was so quiet. That was when I told him of the tragic events that had taken place on the day of his last visit, culminating in Robbie's death in Peachester.

I could not help weeping while I told the story, and Will held my hand, patting and stroking it to console me. When I had finished, we sat silently for a time and then, turning to me with a perplexed expression, he said, "You say that your Mama took Robbie to a doctor in Peachester?"

"Yes," I confirmed, "she took Vicky with her too. But only Mama and Vicky came back, I'm sorry to say."

"And your Mama left Robbie with this doctor? In his care? Until Thursday, when he died?"

"She did her best for him, Will," I answered, sensing that he was accusing Mama of not doing enough for the little one.

Now Will turned to face me directly. "Sarah," he said, "I think you are mistaken. You see, there is no doctor in Peachester — apart from the odd traveling quack."

I could hardly believe my ears. How could this boy, who only visited on weekends and who had known nothing of the circumstances of

Robbie's death until I had told him five minutes before, have the insensitivity to make such a statement? As if I could forget where the child had died. Worse, I could not ignore the implication that Mama had lied.

"Of course there's a doctor in Peachester. Where else would Mama have taken him? Not all the way to Ipswich. He might have died there and then, had he been subjected to a long journey like that!"

"Sarah," Will replied, his voice calm and steady, "my Uncle Bertie has the ague, you know — the shakes — and he has to go to Ipswich for his treatment for the very reason that I have just given. There is no doctor in Peachester. If you don't believe me, go and ask Uncle. It is his constant wish that there was."

"Then I will ask Mama again," I answered. "Now let the subject drop."

But I confess that I never did ask Mama. Partly, I think, because I was too afraid of what her answer might be.

3

THE STUFF OF DREAMS

Mama always referred to me as a "daydreamer," chiefly because of my habit of drifting away into reverie instead of getting on with the washing or the sweeping or whatever other task she had allocated to me — but about the time that little Robbie was taken from us, I began to dream in earnest. My nightly sleep was filled with images of pale and ghostly children climbing in and out of trains, and I was glad when morning came.

As we slept under such crowded conditions, it was common for me to go to bed at the same time as the little ones in order to avoid disturbing them. Ben and Horace were bedded down in a cupboard-sized space beside the kitchen (I had reason to believe it had once been the pantry). Vicky slept in a crib beside Mama — where Robbie had once slept when he was the "newest" baby — while Maggie and Josephine and I shared the front room across the hall.

Since Mama insisted upon practicing the motto "early to bed, early to rise," it was usual for me to be awake while the girls were soundly sleeping in their little beds. It was during this time, before I fell asleep myself, that I would lie and think.

My bed was beside the front window. Above me, through the threadbare curtains, I could see the full panoply of the velvet sky in all its starry glory. There were times when this vision lifted me from my thoughts of the mundane tasks of my day, tempting me to hope that, one day, I too would be as bright and beautiful as the stars that I gazed upon. More often, though, the sight of their beauty reduced me to tears, so hopeless did my future appear.

When I did eventually sleep, the dreams would come. Sometimes I dreamt of the young woman at the station. I saw her alight from the carriage and give her baby to Mama while I stood by, immobile as a statue. But when the train moved off, and the smoke and steam had cleared, I was no longer standing there — rather, it was myself in Mama's arms, my own face peering out from that bonnet and rug, and the woman who gazed back from the departing carriage was weeping for me. For me! And always, upon this discovery, I awoke.

There was, however, another dream which was much more pleasant. In this I walked the swampland with Will. There was always just the two of us, no little ones to be seen or heard at all, and while he told me of the flora that abounded in that place, I gathered what I could in order to preserve and mount it. Although this dream was quite wonderful, the curious thing about it was that not a word was actually spoken by either of us; that is, although we appeared to be talking, throughout the entire dream no sound came from our lips. Yet I understood, almost intuitively, what Will was saying — even about to say — as if I knew the names and characteristics of the plants before he spoke of them.

The daytime outcome of this particular dream was to make me wish, all the more, that I might be allowed to return to the swamp — a desire which Mama vehemently denied. "Why?" she demanded when I persisted. "You have already been there once with that boy."

"His name is Will," I brazenly reminded her. "And that time I took all the little ones, just to make you happy, if you remember." Very rarely did I find the courage to test Mama's patience, but on this issue I was determined to have my way. "You can go off alone any time you like, but I am with the children every single moment, day and night. Am I never to be allowed to do anything without them?"

Whether Mama was taken aback by my reasoning or by my foolhardiness in standing up for myself, I could not tell, but I noticed her expression change, her denial weaken a little, though she did not break altogether. "Listen to me, Missy," she continued, "I will not have it said about town that Mama Pratchett's children wander the streets like homeless waifs."

Had I not been so angry I would have laughed, but that I dared not do. Mama's sense of humor, limited as it was, had never included the ability to laugh at herself, let alone to be laughed at! So I contented myself with replying, "Mama, there is one street in Waterford, and if we wander that like waifs, it is only because we are dressed in other children's castoffs, while you go about like the Queen!" That remark earned me a cuff on the ear!

Still, in the weeks which followed, I was not put off. Rather, I changed my tactics from badgering and insolence to deliberate subservience. There was no household task too mean for me to undertake. Indeed, I cheerfully volunteered for most, and in advance. The daily emptying of our chamber pots was carried out immediately the last warm bottoms had risen from them; the contents of the iron drum in the outdoor latrine were disposed of judiciously before the slightest odor could taint a nostril or a single fly buzz about the user's head. Never, not even had she been mistress of the noblest household, could Mama have expected more of the lowliest downstairs maid. At length, my apparent devotion reaped its reward.

One morning, over a breakfast of over-salted porridge with water, Mama poured herself a cup of tea, stirred in her three sugars (our porridge had none), then sat back and said, "You know, Missy, I sometimes wonder what I would have done if you hadn't come along."

This statement struck me as particularly odd. First, that it should be said at all, since it was very nearly a compliment. Second, to the best of my knowledge, babies didn't just "come along" — unless, of course, they were dropped off from trains like Vicky, who lay in her crib on the floor beside me, cheerily gurgling over a crust.

"Mama?" I said, as an encouragement for her to continue.

"Well, Missy, I suppose there's no harm in letting you go down to the swamp alone.

Heaven knows, nobody else goes there. But the question is, why would you want to?"

I knew then that my strategy had been successful and saw no reason not to tell the truth. "It's a wonderful place, Mama," I told her. "The space, the pools, but especially the wildflowers that grow there. They're quite different from your garden flowers. These are not pretty pink and lavender. And not at all showy. Many of them are so plain and simple, and with their colors of russets and browns, you can hardly see them among the foliage. So, Mama, I was wanting to go down and pick some, then press them, and start a little collection, you see? I was just beginning to do that the night you came back from Robbie's doctor in Peachester, remember? But because of the bad news ..."

She was looking at me in such a peculiar way that I left off, thinking perhaps I had been too presumptuous and she had no intention of letting me go at all.

"And where did this idea come from?" she asked cautiously.

I admit that I was confused. "Why, me, Mama. It was my idea. I thought that it would be —"

This time she held up her hand to cut me off. "And nobody else's?"

"No, Mama."

"Just something you dreamed up, eh?"

Her reference to my dreams was astonishing. Mama often said that she knew me "inside out," but to know my dreams was uncanny, so much so that I felt my cheeks burn, though why they should was equally a mystery. After all, why couldn't I dream?

"Mama, how ..." I began, but she gave me one last suspicious look and got up from the table.

"You can go, I suppose. This morning, if you like. But not until this kitchen is cleaned up and the washing done. And then only for an hour. I don't want to be running about the town organizing a search party to drag the swamp. Then there'd be trouble. Serious trouble. Do you understand, Missy?"

"Yes, Mama," I replied meekly, since I understood only too well.

Later that morning I set out alone for the swamp. I cannot adequately express how excited I was to be alone at last, but having climbed the stile, I found myself almost overcome with panic at the limitless prospect of the landscape that lay before me. I chose the same route that Will had shown us, considering it wiser to take the known path than have myself fall into an abandoned peat pit or some other unknown danger. Still, it was not the same, traversing the area without the guidance of Will and the happy voices of the children.

The morning was gray and overcast, and somehow the utter silence of the place filled me with a sense of foreboding. I had the most peculiar feeling that I was not alone. I tried to put this behind me, constantly telling myself that I was foolish and even attempting an airy whistle to give myself confidence. But the feeling persisted and finally I turned, assuming that one of the children had followed me. "Maggie?" I called. "Ben?" But when no answer came I stopped in my tracks and reproached myself with: Missy, you've been longing for this opportunity, now take it. And so I gripped Mama's pruning shears more tightly, tightened the strings of my bonnet, and went on, my lips pursed and my brow furrowed in determination.

The flowers that I had seen some weeks before were still in profusion, and I set about gathering them with a will. The more I gathered, the more my fears slipped away. I found a clump of tallow-colored flags here, a cluster of ground-hugging honeydews there, brown boronia in a little clearing, and even a clump of wood violets nestled beneath a rotting log. On seeing these, I laid my specimens on the ground beside me and knelt to pick them. As I did so, I experienced the sensation that I was being observed.

I turned cautiously to check. There in the clearing behind me stood a woman, her head and shoulders lit by a sun ray that had momentarily burst through a parting in the clouds.

I was so astonished that I fell back, my legs folding beneath me. "Who are you?" I gasped, but the woman neither answered nor made any attempt to come closer. "What do you want?" I asked, my voice sounding nervous and shrill, but still she did not reply, and if she moved at all, it was only to incline her head a little more, the better to stare down at me.

I thought that perhaps she had also been rambling and had lost her way — that perhaps she was as surprised to encounter me as I her. She certainly seemed to be dressed for a walk. She held a deep green parasol over her shoulder and wore an elegant, though sensible, straw hat with a gauze veil which obscured her face. Her dress was of fine butter-colored muslin, falling softly to brush the instep of her buttoned boots.

Sensing that she had no intention of speaking or advancing towards me, I got to my feet, straightened my ragged skirt, and said, "I'm Sarah. I was gathering flowers. The violets here, you see? Are you lost? Can I help you?" At this, she took a step forward and held out her gloved hand towards me, which I hesitatingly took, feeling the suppleness of soft leather. "Do you want me to guide you?" I asked, but she shook her head then, glancing over her shoulder as if she too were being watched. She squeezed my fingers firmly — as a sign of reassurance, I imagined — then she vanished.

I say "vanished" because there is no other word to describe her departure. One second she was there, holding my hand, and the next she was gone, leaving me alone and trembling. I ran at once through the clearing and looked down the rough pathway that led away from it, but I could see no one. I called, my voice sounding high and foolish, "Are you there?" but no answer came. In utter confusion I even ran to the bank of the reedy waters that stretched the length of the path, but all I could see was a phantom twist of vapor that rose from their surface towards the strengthening sun.

Now I was truly afraid. That she had been there, I could not doubt. The softness of her touch remained with me still. The image of her figure, every detail of what she had worn, was so clear to me, but she simply was not there.

In order to assure myself that I had not been dreaming — or worse, losing my sanity — I searched the muddy pathway for the imprint of her boot, some definite and visible sign, but there was nothing, and I dropped my head into my hands.

When I had settled myself I hurried back to where I had left my specimens, not bothering to gather the wood violets that I had been about to pick, and set out for home, my mind still filled with every possibility that only a child's imagination can conjure. And, worst of all, who was there to share my fears with? If I should tell Mama, I should never be allowed to leave her again. If I told any of the little ones, I would only provoke nightmares and long sleepless nights as I comforted them.

And then the answer came to me — if I told anyone, it should be Will Quaver! Will, who was always sensible. Will, who knew the swampland like the back of his hand.

4

A FRIENDSHIP BLOSSOMS

When I returned home that day I hid my reactions to the appearance of the woman with the parasol by devoting what spare time I had to pressing my flowers. Again I took papers from Mama's room, put the blooms between their pages, and pressed them beneath the panes of glass that I had found in the yard. This being done, and conscious that the last time my efforts had been destroyed, I placed the specimens beneath my bed where they could not be interfered with or damaged. There they remained until Will came down.

I admit to feeling more than a trifle foolish, telling him of what I had seen in the swamp, and I fully expected him to laugh at my story, but, Will being Will, he did not. Rather, he listened intently and nodded encouragingly for me to continue. When at last I had finished

I asked, "Well? Do you think that I am just a silly child, or could I have seen something — you know — something supernatural?"

"Sarah," he began, rubbing his chin as if he were an ancient sage, "I would have to reserve judgment—"

"So," I exclaimed, "you do think I am being silly. You think I'm just making up ghost stories, don't you?"

"Don't be foolish. What I meant was that I would have to reserve judgment on the nature of the woman that you saw. The world is a strange place, Sarah, and my Uncle Bertie says that there's room in it for both the living and the dead. It's just that the dead, being spirits, don't take up so much space, which is very convenient and considerate for the living, you see? So, no, I don't think you're silly at all. In fact, I'd like very much to go to the swamp with you, just in case she returns. But there is one thing that I have to be sure of, if you don't mind answering a very personal question?"

I was instantly suspicious. "That depends."

"Well, have you been rude or nasty to a woman who fits the description of the one that you saw recently? That is, in the last six months or so, do you remember? One carrying a parasol, perhaps? Or wearing kid gloves?"

I did not need to give this question much thought. When was I likely to encounter a woman of such elegance in Waterford? And why, if I ever did, would I have been rude to her? More likely I would faint dead away, thinking that she was a princess of the realm.

"No," I answered. "Why?"

"Well, if you had seen such a woman, and had upset her in some way, and she had subsequently died, it could be — now I'm not saying that this is a certainty, merely a possibility — that she had come back to haunt you. Or so my uncle says, and he is station master, you know."

I was unsure how Will's uncle's elevated status in the railway could contribute to his knowledge of the spiritual world, but was satisfied that I had learned all I could from Will on the subject of my apparition, so I led him into the house to see my collection of pressed flowers.

"They should have been under pressure for long enough," I told him as I drew the glass out and placed it flat on my bed. "Are you ready to see?"

When he nodded, we took hold of the top sheet of glass and lifted it from the papers beneath. This done, I drew off each sheet of paper ever so carefully until, at last, the flowers lay exposed before us. But I could not hide my disappointment at what was revealed.

"Oh, Will," I exclaimed when I saw their drab petals. "They were rich russets and velvety browns and the mossiest greens. Now they've lost their color altogether. What can I do?"

"Well, at least I can still recognize what they are, but then, I don't know what you were expecting, what you were trying to achieve."

"I wanted to preserve them just as they were. As glowing and special as the day that I picked them, that's what. These — well, they look plain dead ..."

He attempted to pick up one of the blooms, but it broke into pieces the moment it was lifted from the paper. Will sat on the bed with a sigh. "Hmmm, then it looks as if you're going to have to try another way if it's life and color you want."

"What other way?" I asked eagerly, thinking that he was about to introduce me to some new technique of preservation.

Instead, he said simply, "You could paint them."

"That's silly," I laughed. "How could anyone paint this?" I crumbled one of the brittle flowers in my fingers. "Why, it won't bear touching, let alone painting!"

"I meant that you could paint a picture of them. Actually, draw them, then paint them. And if you did, the paintings would be so much easier to mount and frame than a whole pile of separate flowers. How about that?"

"Me? Be an artist?" I scoffed, though the idea was immediately exciting to me. "What would Mama have to say about that? It was hard enough getting permission to gather them, let alone to spend time painting them!"

"That's a difficulty you will have to overcome, Sarah," he said, and I knew from the tone of his voice and the look in his eye that he was quite serious. "You have to start standing up for yourself sometime. How many other girls your age are left in charge of a family while their mother gads about every railway station in the state? It's just not fair."

I had no argument to counter this, so I chose to take a different tack. "Even if I did decide to paint them," I said, folding my arms, "where, pray, would I get the money to buy the paints? Not from Mama, I assure you!"

"What? She gives you no money of your own?"

"No."

"Not even for all the work you do around the house?"

Now it was my turn to sigh. "Will, Mama has no money. She's a seamstress. Do you know what a seamstress earns? And she hasn't got a husband to support her ..." I almost added "as she would like," but Will suddenly broke into a laugh, which stopped me.

"Well, it looks as though she's trying hard to find one," he said, tapping his finger on one of the sheets of newspaper.

"What?"

"Here, see?" He held the paper up to reveal a series of neat rectangular holes that had been cut in it. "This is the Personal column. It's where lonely gentlemen advertise for home help or even a woman who might want to be their bride. I'd say Mama's doing a bit more than going to the markets when she goes to town!"

This proposition was so preposterous that I snatched the paper from him to look for myself. What Will said was true. The column was labeled "Personal" and there were the advertisements that had been entered by men seeking female companionship. As if to convince myself, I began to read some aloud:

"'Hard-working widower with established home. No children. Non-smoker, non-drinker. Requires middle-aged lady to share his life. Contact "Widower." Post Office, Range View.'

"Here's another:

"'Stonemason. 35 years. Losing hope of finding wife. Steady and of good character. Contact Mr. Brown. Charlottesville Cemetery.'"

Will put an eye to one of the holes before I could go on. "I told you so," he said cheekily. "Now what do you think of dear Mama? Maybe that's the reason she always leaves dressed up to the nines. Why, even today, didn't I catch her getting on the train all done up in red. Red! Of all colors, Missy!"

To say that I was flabbergasted would be an understatement. Mama, out shopping for a man! Our Mama! But what could I say to deny the possibility? Certainly the clippings had not been removed from the paper by one of the children — the cutting out was too tidily executed for that. What other explanation could there be? Unless Will was in error. Unless there were other advertisements: positions vacant, perhaps for a seamstress? That could also explain why Mama had dressed so well. But short of a dozen other requests for wives, and one for a husband, I could find nothing else that Mama might have replied to.

My alternatives were at an end. "I'm sorry, Will," I said, crestfallen, "it looks as if you're right. And I thought that I knew Mama so well, but now ... This is awful."

"I don't know," he replied, wise to the end. "It could all work out for the good. If your Mama does find somebody, I think she would be canny enough to choose a worthwhile somebody. You know, I'm certain that Uncle Bertie would snap her up in a minute if he wasn't so shy. It's his funny voice, you see. He doesn't like talking very much. But I've seen the way he looks at her and he's always asking me about her — like is there a Mr. Pratchett and all. So who knows? You might turn out to have a decent father after all. And have a little money in your pocket for those paints. But I've really got to go, my train leaves in half an hour. If it's any consolation, I'd be putting my money on Mama. Bye!"

5

THE MOTHER'S FRIEND

As summer drew to a close, the cold, damp winds of approaching autumn crept from the swamplands into our shack. Try as we might, we could not keep them out. Mama's Sunday papers were again put to good use, stuffed under doors, wedged into cracks in windows, even spread beneath our mattresses to keep the drafts out, but all to no avail.

"We should be prepared for a spate of early colds, I'm afraid, Missy," Mama said to me one particularly chilly evening as we bedded the children down. "I think that I've already heard the odd wheeze from Horace. It is a concern."

I personally thought that Horrie had never looked better. His cheeks had the rosiest glow and his eyes were bright as buttons, but on the subject of threatened illness I had learned never to contradict. Mama had an uncanny knack of detecting the earliest symptoms, which invariably developed into a life-threatening malady within days.

When this occurred, Mama resorted to her favorite remedy, "Mother Hibberd's Soothing Syrup" or, as she called it, "The Mother's Friend." To her this was a cure-all and a household essential. Horrie was immediately dosed with it in an effort to fend off his approaching cold. After a week of this treatment I thought that he seemed worse than before — certainly he was more prone to tears and melancholy, and he often drifted off to sleep with his little fist stuck in his mouth and his cheeks damp with tears.

There was another peculiarity about Horrie's condition that I noticed. While Mama assiduously supervised my twice-daily administration of his syrup, not once did she take him in her arms when he became tired and wan, or console him when he was petulant. Rather, she seemed to grow less and less tolerant of his presence, shouting for me to "Do something about that child!" or "Take that sniveling boy away before he passes whatever it is he has on to Victoria!"

But it was Mama herself who caught Horrie's

"infection" — as she called it. And yet the very week that she became ill she had insisted on taking the train to Ipswich on a heavy and overcast day and was obliged to return, without an umbrella, in the pouring rain.

At first she was generally irritable, but none of us paid too much attention to that because it was almost second nature to her. Then she began to sniffle and sneeze. This she put down to hay fever, although it was autumn and there was hardly a pollen-bearing flower to be found. It was only when her body ached so much that she simply could not go on that she acknowledged she was ill and must stay in her bed.

This was the first time in my memory that such a thing had happened to Mama. It meant that the full responsibility for the running of the house fell on me. In itself this was not unusual. I was used to preparing the meals and doing the washing and cleaning but, up until this time, Mama had always done the marketing. Now, however, she was too sick to leave the house and, short of having us all starve, herself included, she was forced to allow me to go. More importantly, she was forced to trust me with money.

I had always known that we were miserably poor, but it was not until Mama sat me down on the side of her bed and gave me a half-crown from her purse that I understood how serious our situation was. "Here, Missy," she said, reluctantly putting the coin in my palm and closing my fingers over it, "this will have to do for your train fare to Peachester, some groceries, and a bottle of 'Mother's Friend.' Your fare should be sixpence return, the syrup a shilling, which leaves you three and sixpence for the food. Get milk powder and rusks for Victoria before you buy anything else. Remember what the children eat and what will go around, so don't be buying anything frivolous."

"Mama," I said, "I will be lucky to buy anything at all with three and six, won't I? And with you being so sick, shouldn't I try to get some fresh fruit? Some oranges or lemons?"

"No. If I need to, I will take a little 'Mother's Friend' myself. In fact, while you're in town, get two bottles. I think the time has come to increase Horace's dose."

"But Mama," I protested, "it doesn't seem to be doing him any good at all. It just seems to make him drowsy and dull. If the day is fine, could I rug him up and take him with me? Maybe he should see little Robbie's doctor—"

"A doctor?" she barked. "See a doctor for a bit of a cold? What, do you think money grows on trees? Have you seen me sewing lately?"

"No, Mama."

"So where do you think the money for this doctor is coming from, eh? Or is that what you were looking for on your mysterious expedition into the swamp, eh? Looking for a money tree, perhaps?"

My hour of freedom had never been forgotten and would long be held over me. "No, Mama," I answered meekly, afraid that if I upset her further I would never be allowed to go again. "It's just that I'm worried that the syrup is making Horrie worse."

"Rubbish. It's a godsend. And what would a bit of a Miss like you know, anyway? Now, there's a train leaving for Peachester at nine o'clock. That gives you half an hour. And there's another returning at midday. So off you go."

"But Mama," I said, beginning to tremble, "I've never done this before. I don't know anything about the markets in Peachester. How will I know where to go or what to do? And the train ..."

It is quite possible that Mama had not realized my lack of experience in dealing with the outside world, although it was nobody's fault but her own. Still, she showed me little mercy. "What is there to know, Miss? You go to the station and buy a return ticket to Peachester, child's fare. The train comes and you get on it. You get off at Peachester and the grocer's market is right in front of you. You buy what you need and come home. Is that so difficult for a girl your age?"

This much I accepted, but in spite of her rising anger I asked, "And the syrup? Where do I buy that?"

She looked at me as if I were a simpleton. "At the same place, of course."

"At the market?"

"Where else?"

"But isn't it from a pharmacist?"

Here she frowned and paused before answering. "No," she said flatly.

"But Mama, it is proper medicine, isn't it?" Knowing that I was entering dangerous ground, I edged away from the bed. "Don't I need a prescription?"

"No," she mumbled, rearranging her bedclothes to avoid my gaze. "Just tell the grocer that you're picking it up for Mrs. Pratchett. That's all you need to know."

"Mama, it isn't some concoction made by a traveling quack, is it? Mixed up out of herbs and leaves in the back of a caravan? You told us that gypsies do that, don't you remember?"

At this she puffed herself up and looked me straight in the eye. "You really are an impudent little Miss, aren't you? As if your Mama would be giving some gypsy elixir to her babies. Why, I'm even thinking of taking it myself. Now, off you go. I've heard enough of your whining for one day."

I left for the station rugged up in an overcoat that had seen better days. I wore black woolen stockings that Mama had darned so many times and in so many colors they might suit a harlequin. I had a moth-eaten beret pulled down on my head, and for good measure I carried a string bag and an enormous black umbrella that Mama had bought second-hand at a charity bazaar. With the recent altercation still heavy in my heart, and outfitted so hideously, I hardly felt prepared for my first train journey alone, even though it would last only fifteen minutes. I felt a sudden longing for Will and regretted that it was not Saturday, when I could have found solace in the company of someone my own age.

In this melancholy mood I trudged to the station and mounted the stairs that led to the ticket office. I drew the half-crown that Mama had given me from the inner pocket of my coat and was about to hand it to old Mr. Quaver when he said, "Where is your Mama?"

"Mama's sick," I answered, "so I'm going into Peachester to buy the groceries."

"Sick, is she?"

"Yes," I said. "But I'm going to buy her some medicine."

"Medicine, eh? That sick, is she?"

"I think it's a bad cold, Mr. Quaver. It seems to have gone down onto her chest."

"On her chest, eh?"

Each of these repetitions was accompanied by a long and studied stare which I found most disconcerting, and finally I was obliged to say, "Could I please have my ticket, Mr. Quaver? I'm certain that I can hear the train coming."

These words were hardly out of my mouth when a hand fell on my shoulder. I spun around, thinking that some ruffian was about to relieve me of Mama's precious money, and there stood Will, his smile wide and cheeky, his hair as flaming and erratic as ever.

"What are you doing here?" I gasped.

"Got bored at school, didn't I? Thought I'd drop down to see Missy Sarah for a three-day weekend. How does that sound?"

"Wonderful," I said, though I would not admit to thinking about him, considering him egotistical enough. "But I have to go into Peachester now. The train is due at any minute."

Will was not concerned at all. "Great," he said, grabbing my elbow. "In that case I'll go with you. And you can put your money back in your pocket."

"Will," I protested, pulling away, "I have to buy a ticket."

"No, you don't. Uncle Bertie will let us on for nothing. In the guard's van. That's the way I always travel. Besides, then you get to save your sixpence. You can spend it in town."

Remembering the little that I had been given to spend on food, I was delighted to accept his offer, though the prospect of traveling in the guard's van without a ticket frightened me. I had heard countless stories from Mama about people who were caught cheating on fares and thrown off trains in the most godforsaken places.

"You're sure we will be all right?" I asked, for which I earned a stern talking-to.

"Now, Missy," he said, "have I ever let you down? Or is it that you doubt the influence of the Quaver name on the Ipswich line? Tell me, which?"

When Will behaved like this I could only laugh, and soon my fears were lost as we rattled towards Peachester, sitting on top of a cage of hens while the guard read his newspaper, paying us no more attention than if we had been a pair of Rhode Island Reds ourselves. We certainly cackled enough.

It wasn't that I hadn't been shopping before. At Christmas, Mama would bend her rules and take us all out for a treat, but that hour I spent in Peachester with Will was far better than any Yuletide excursion. And while it is true that I had nothing to buy but groceries and soothing syrup, Will even made that exciting. He invented games for every occasion: to see who could find the pumpkin most likely to become Cinderella's carriage, the particular lima bean that was certain to sprout all the way up to Jack the Giant Killer's castle above the clouds, even the very pea that kept the Princess awake upon her mountain of mattresses — although opening the pods for this latter contest earned us a scowl from the grocer's wife. But, best of all, Will stayed with me the entire time, talking and laughing, until I had all but forgotten my troubles. Until I had everything but the soothing syrup, that is.

"Soothing syrup?" he repeated. "What's soothing syrup?"

"It's a remedy for colds and sore throats and other chest complaints," I explained. "Mama believes in it implicitly."

"I've never heard of it. Does it work?"

"Mama seems to think so."

"Seems to think so? That doesn't sound like a recommendation."

"Well ..." I answered hesitantly, unwilling to cast doubts upon Mama's medical expertise. "In my opinion, it's not worth much at all. That is" — I gathered courage from my friend's look of concern — "if Horrie's condition is any example ..."

"What? My friend Horrie? Is he sick then?"

"Yes."

Will stopped mid-stride. "But Sarah, you only lost little Robbie two months ago. It's not the same thing, is it?"

"No, no," I assured him. "Robbie died of the meningitis. Horrie's just a little off-color, that's all. It's nothing to worry about, I'm sure. Besides, it's Mama who's really sick. The syrup is for her. So don't worry ..."

I was acutely aware as I said this that I was not telling the whole truth, but the thought of returning home without the syrup was too terrible to contemplate. I quickly went up to the counter and requested it, adding in a lower voice so that Will could not hear me, "Make that two bottles please," then standing away the moment that they were wrapped and paid for.

"Well," I announced, "that's all the shopping done. Should we be heading back to the station, then?"

"When were you supposed to be home?" Will asked, checking the time by the clock in the square.

"I was catching the twelve noon."

"Then we've got a good forty-five minutes to have a look around town. Maybe even buy a sherbet cone. Have you still got the sixpence you didn't spend on your fare?"

I checked my pocket and found that I had a sixpenny piece, three pennies and a halfpenny: ninepence ha'penny in all. A fortune by my standards.

"An excellent demonstration of household economy, m'dear," Will congratulated me playfully. "Does that mean two sherbet cones, or something even more adventurous? A box of French truffles perhaps? Very la-di-dah ..."

I couldn't help smiling at his antics, but the thought of spending the money on anything "frivolous," as Mama had warned, could not have been further from my mind. "No, Will, I'd rather go back to the market and get some fruit for Mama and the little ones. I saw some oranges there that were as bright as your hair." This was said in an attempt to amuse him, but his smile faded so quickly that I assumed my remark had been too personal and that I had offended him. "I'm sorry, Will," I spluttered. "Really. I didn't mean ..."

"Don't say sorry to me," he said sternly. "It's yourself that you should feel sorry for. Here you are with the chance to buy something special, some little treat worth threepence maybe, and you won't even allow yourself to do that. It's always Mama and the little ones, isn't it? Truly, Sarah, I don't know how you do it."

I started to feel my temper rise as he said this. How I spent Mama's hard-earned money was none of his business, but I bit my tongue in the interest of our friendship. "Will, I've tried to explain before that we don't have any money. If I buy myself a sherbet, and I'd really like to, how could I go home and face the little ones with a clear conscience? Will, I simply can't."

Perhaps he finally understood my situation, I couldn't tell, but at least he gave me a conciliatory smile. Taking the string bag of groceries, he said, "Come on then, Missy, at least you can afford to go window shopping, eh what?"

Again Will made this a source of fun and we laughed as if we had never argued, but I thought that he did seem to be hurrying unduly until we stopped dead before a stationery supplier's window and he covered his mouth, gasping. "Why! Did you ever see such a fine box of paints!"

I told him that I had not.

"And only a florin. So reasonably priced, too."

They could have been worth five pounds so far as I was concerned, since I was never likely to own them. But Will had put the string bag down on the pavement and was deeply involved in the process of emptying his trouser pockets. I saw him withdraw a handful of coins of varying denominations, none higher than a sixpence, before he muttered, "Yes, by jingo. I've just got enough. Come on ..." And before I could say a word he picked up the groceries and went into the shop.

"That box of watercolors in the window," he said to the white-coated assistant, "might I see it, please?"

The assistant reached in, removed the box, and placed it squarely on the glass-topped counter before Will.

"What do you think?" he asked me, opening

it to display a dozen squares of brilliant paints. "And see? There are two good brushes as well."

"It's beautiful, Will, really it is. If you have the money, get it. I would, if you know what I mean."

"I know exactly what you mean, Missy. And, just to prove that I do, I'll take your advice."

With that, he released the coins in his hand onto the counter, where they fell with a clatter. "You'll find that's the correct money," he said to the assistant in a matter-of-fact voice. "And we'll have it wrapped, please. And, if you don't mind, you can throw in a sheet or two of nice white paper, as goodwill, you know."

I saw the assistant hesitate a moment, then break into a smile. "Certainly, sir," he said. "Anything for a budding young artist like yourself."

But Will grew suddenly serious and, leaning forwards as if to share a confidence, he said, "No, my friend. You are mistaken. It's the young lady who's the budding artist. The paints are for her."

When the paints were wrapped and I had finished thanking Will, we still had time to buy some oranges.

6

A SECRET
IN THE GARDEN

The weeks that followed my visit to Peachester are among the worst in my memory. Mama's illness turned out to be little more than a common cold, although to listen to her moaning, anyone would have believed that she was in the final throes of consumption. Throughout this period her temper was ready to flare at the slightest provocation and her demands for me to wait upon her every request, with no regard for whatever else I might be doing, were intolerable. While I know that she did have the sniffles, was most likely running a temperature, and probably had a constant headache, I think that what concerned her most was that no sewing work was coming in and, as a result, we had no money.

Perhaps it was because of the lack of parcels arriving for Mama — or, possibly, her failure to turn up regularly at the station — that Mr. Quaver paid his first visit.

It was a miserably wet day and I was hanging some diapers out to dry under cover of our veranda roof when I caught sight of a tall, thin figure dressed in a black raincoat and hunched under an enormous black umbrella coming from the station. I could not make out who it was at first, but when he came closer and the wind momentarily lifted the umbrella from his face, I could tell that it was Old Bertie, as we had come to call him — though I confess that he was probably no more than fifty years old, as was Mama. To see him away from the station — and approaching our house, at that — was unusual to say the least.

I did not look at him directly. Rather, I partially turned my back and pretended to be absorbed in my work, though all the while I was watching him from the corner of my eye. When I saw that it was his intention to turn in at our gate, I realized that I must warn Mama, who was sound asleep in her bedroom, snoring her head off. In order to prevent drawing attention to this plan, I moved along the length of the clothesline, all the while checking that the diapers were firmly pegged, until I reached her bedroom window, which I rapped upon as hard as I could.

After much "rat-a-tat-tatting" on my part, I heard her mumble, "What? What? You pest of a girl," and I was able to lean down and indicate by sign language that we were about to have a visitor.

I must say that I was very glad that I did this, as was Mama, since to see her mountainous form in a nightdress (especially by day) was not the most pleasant of sights — particularly if it was her intention to impress a prospective suitor, as I had begun to suspect Old Bertie to be. My warning came just in time. No sooner had Mama rolled off her bed and begun hastily to dress than Bertie was at our gate, calling out to me, "Miss Pratchett? Miss Pratchett?" in his high-pitched voice.

"Good afternoon, Mr. Quaver," I replied, and stepped off the veranda to meet him as quickly as I could — as much to allow Mama more time to make herself presentable as to prevent him from bursting my eardrums by calling out again. "What can I do for you?"

"Your Mama still not well, eh?" he asked, lowering his voice a little as I approached.

"No, she's not at all well," I said, hoping that statement might serve as a deterrent to his coming any closer.

"So she's at home, is she? In the house, eh?"

I must say that, apart from the day I had been

to Peachester and seen him through the grille of the ticket office, this was the closest I had ever been to Old Bertie, and I was pleasantly surprised by his appearance. Although his skin was yellow and wrinkled as a walnut, he had the most kindly gray eyes, and while his face was thin, it was nevertheless well formed: his jaw square and his nose as straight as if it had been chiseled for a Hermes or an Achilles. When he folded his umbrella, I couldn't help but note that his hands were as fine a work of nature's art as I had seen on any man — though I confess to knowing very few!

"Yes, Mr. Quaver," I answered. "Would you come in and wait on our veranda out of the rain while I fetch her?"

"Ah," he said, showing some surprise. "So she's not confined to her bed, eh?"

Hearing Mama clumping about in her room like a cow, I assumed that she was almost ready and so I lied, saying, "Well, although she's poorly, you can't keep a good woman down, can you?"

"No, no," he agreed with much nodding, "that you cannot. And she's a good woman, sure enough. They don't come any better, eh?"

Since one barefaced lie a day was more than my usual quota, I refrained from answering this in the affirmative. Rather, I lowered my head and led our guest up the rough path to the front stairs of the veranda, where I turned to him and took his dripping coat, hanging it over the clothesline there. This being done, I asked him to wait a moment and slipped into the house to find Mama.

I found her bustling around in her bedroom, searching for a missing shoe. "It's Mr. Quaver," I whispered, "from the station."

She paused in her rooting under the bed just long enough to spit back at me, "I know that, you silly girl! Do you think I didn't see him through the window? Now don't stand there like a stuffed duck! Help me here."

I found the missing shoe among the piles of bedclothes that had tumbled to the floor, and when I had helped stuff her foot into it (feeling a little like Cinderella dressing one of her ugly sisters), I managed to stick one or two hairpins into her bun before pushing her through the door.

Never have I seen such a transformation. If Old Bertie had come expecting to see a woebegone and suffering woman, he found himself struck by a sunbeam. Mama was a picture of light and air, her welcoming smile fit to stir the heart of the most confirmed bachelor.

"Why, Mrs. Pratchett," Bertie chirped, his voice at least an octave higher than usual, "here I was believing you to be laid low, but I find you up and about. And what a pleasure, eh? What a pleasure."

I doubt that Mama had heard him say as many words together in her life, but as usual she was equal to the situation. "Why, Mr. Quaver," she answered, batting her eyelids as she held a hand to her ample breast, "you do flatter me."

I was not entirely sure that Old Bertie had flattered her, but having been told that he had, he seemed to gather more confidence in stating the purpose of his visit. "Well, I have only come to inquire after your health, Ma'am," he proceeded, "and to offer my services to you should you need them during your time of indisposition. Not that you appear to be ill, I hasten to say; indeed you seem the very picture of health, but such is your strength of character, I am certain of it. Your strength of character, eh?"

Had somebody said this to me, I might well have taken offense. Not that you appear to be ill, indeed! But I doubt that the poor man knew what he was saying, with Mama standing there fanning her breast with a handkerchief and cooing like a pouter pigeon!

"Oh," she sighed, "do come again, Mr. Quaver. But next time, perhaps, could you send down that dear nephew of yours first? Just to be certain that I am able to receive—" Here she positively erupted with the most frightful paroxysms of bronchial coughs, sufficient to blow the man away. Then, covering her mouth with the handkerchief, she managed to gasp, "You see, there are entire days when I am simply too weak ..." She was in the process of drawing a tubercular breath and about to erupt again when he turned and hurried down the stairs.

"Oh, certainly," he called, partway to the gate, "oh, certainly ..." though as Mama saw that he was leaving so soon, she successfully stifled the pending cough and managed a wave which might have served as the parting gesture of a mother seeing her only son off to war.

"Stupid man," Mama muttered as she turned indoors. "Make sure you keep him away in future. You know how I hate people nosing about ... Unless he wants to give us something, of course."

Which is exactly what dear Old Bertie did, although he took care not to disturb Mama. More than once I caught sight of him slipping away, and there on the veranda I would find a bag of potatoes or some fresh fruit, and once even a box of the most beautiful little cakes brought all the way from Ipswich!

At that time we were so poor that one day I saw Mama shake out her handbag in order to gather up the loose coins that fell from it, and I was embarrassed daily at having to add to the Pratchett "tab" at Dibbs's store in order to keep up our supply of milk and bread. It fell to my lot to try to make the best of these terrible times, and I was constantly attempting to conjure up new and nourishing meals out of an empty larder. There was plenty of watery soup made from the dry and knobbly turnips and carrots pulled from our garden.

I thought that the children were wonderful during Mama's illness. Maggie, who was only five, was able to make an imaginative game out of almost any task, no matter how tedious. She took all of the wooden clothespins from their old bucket and laid them out on the floor of our veranda. Next, she sharpened the blue indelible pencil that Mama used to mark our clothes and drew eyes and noses and mouths on them. Then she glued on little tufts of copra mattress stuffing so that it looked like hair, until each peg looked exactly like a little human being.

"Now, Sarah," she informed me with the

utmost seriousness, "in the future, whenever you see me hanging out the washing, you should call me 'Miss Pratchett,' because I am a schoolteacher and these are my students, all standing to attention."

As for Ben, although only four, he could be relied upon to amuse Josephine at any time of day, sitting with her on the veranda or the back steps, telling her stories that he spun out of his head as naturally as a spider weaves its web.

Victoria was never any trouble. She was what anyone would call the "perfect baby" and, as such, was clearly Mama's favorite. In fact, on the days when Mama was feeling a little brighter (although these were few and far between), she would take her "little princess" and sit with her in the sun, cooing to her as if she were her true mother, which I alone knew she was not.

It was dear Horace who suffered most during this time. Although the other children knew better than to make a noise, he simply could not help but attract attention to himself. Since Mama had doubled his dose of the soothing syrup (she had, as yet, taken none herself), Horrie had continued to sink lower and lower into a terrible state of melancholy. Nothing I did to amuse him seemed to lift his spirits. He was often to be found asleep, either curled up in his tiny bed or upon the old settee on the veranda, or even, sometimes, upon the bare floorboards where he had been trying to play. Most often he wandered around the house, grizzling and whining, constantly looking for Mama or myself and asking to be picked up or cuddled. When I had the time I was more than happy to soothe him, but Mama found his demands irritating beyond measure.

"What is wrong with the child?" she would bark, pulling her dressing gown from his clutches. "Missy, get him away from me before I strangle him." At other times she would simply command me to "Give him a dose of 'Mother's Friend' for goodness' sake. At least that will put him to sleep. My head is splitting."

My only relief came on Saturdays when Will visited. He would always play with Horrie, but he noticed that the little boy was growing worse. Then the Saturday came when he leaned over the fence and muttered in my ear, "Sarah, I need to talk to you."

"What about?" I asked, feeling somewhat intimidated by his closeness.

When he whispered, "What's wrong with Horrie," I knew that I should listen.

"Mama is resting," I said, "so you can say

what you like, provided it doesn't upset the children."

As we walked around the back garden, he began: "You remember the day we went to Peachester and you bought the soothing syrup?" he asked.

I had to laugh. "More likely I will remember it as the day we went to Peachester and you bought me the paintbox," I corrected him.

"Well, I mentioned the name of that stuff to my mother and she asked me if you had a prescription from a doctor. Did you?"

"No. Mama said it wasn't necessary to take Horrie to a doctor. She said that he only had a bit of a cold. And besides, she said that I could buy 'Mother's Friend' from the grocer."

"Hmmmm." He scratched the back of his head. "You know, Missy, I really like you and I really like Horrie too, and I don't want to make anyone cranky at me or my mother, but what sort of medicine do grocers sell? I mean, it couldn't be much good, could it?"

I had already come to this conclusion myself, but had been too afraid to say so. Besides, in spite of the facts that stared me in the face, I was loath to let anyone suggest that Mama wasn't doing her best. "Just what are you trying to say, Will Quaver?" I demanded.

"Well, after I told my mother, she went out and checked up on that stuff and she told me to tell you that it's made by some old woman in Ipswich and its chief ingredient is laudanum. There, now I've said it."

I had no idea what he was talking about. "Said what?" I asked, genuinely confused.

Will shook his head. "Sarah," he said, "I think there's something terribly wrong happening in your family. Laudanum is a solution extracted from opium. It's a very dangerous drug. It's true that it can be used as a painkiller, but if it's taken in large quantities — and I saw that you bought two bottles — it can cause serious harm. Especially to a child as young as Horrie. He's hardly more than a baby."

I did not know how to respond, so I fell back upon my standard defense of Mama. "That's ridiculous," I declared. "If I were to believe what you're suggesting, Mama is actually harming Horrie by giving him the syrup. Why, she was actually going to take it—" But I checked myself before I said "herself," knowing that she had not.

"Look, Sarah," poor Will began again. "I'm not trying to cause more trouble for you, honest. I just thought that you should know, that's all. Maybe I'm wrong. Maybe my mother is too. Who knows? But Horrie isn't getting any better, is he? Maybe you should convince your Mama to stop giving him the syrup and see what happens. Or better still, take him to a doctor ... Anyway, let's change the subject. Have you tried out the paints yet? Sarah?"

I refused to answer him and stormed off into the house.

I think that it must be very difficult to be dishonest with yourself for very long; at least I have found it so. At first, I tried to pretend that what Will had told me was just so much rubbish. After all, what would his mother possibly know about raising children compared with Mama? By Will's own admission, she had only raised one when Mama had raised so many. And, what was more, Will's mother had never even seen Horace, so how could she possibly be in a position to pass comment on the nature of his medication?

But during the time I was trying to convince myself of these things, Horrie was growing steadily worse, and as he did, Mama became more irritable, even vicious. Once, when the little fellow tried to slip between Mama and Victoria in the vain hope of being hugged, she slapped him so hard on the cheek that the imprint of her hand remained for hours. "Well, Missy," she sneered at me, "if you gave him more of your time he'd be a lot less liable to hang around demanding mine."

"Mama," I countered, "how can you say so? He only wants a soft word and a little love. Is that too much to ask? Victoria is not the only child in this house, you know." I admit that there were times when my mouth too readily declared the feelings in my heart, but on this occasion I did not regret it, despite the consequences.

"You ungrateful little minx," Mama screeched, her attempt to strike me thwarted only by the fact that she had Victoria on her knee. "How I regret the day that I got you from the—"

I had never heard her go so far before, never heard her give so much away, but I was equal to her, and more than ready to push her to the limit. "Got me from where, Mama?" I taunted. "From the station, were you about to say? Where you got Vicky?"

I believe that she had genuinely frightened herself, but rather than lose face, she screamed, "Get out. Get out of my sight. And take that screaming child with you."

I did as she said, not out of any wish to obey

her, but rather to come to the aid of poor Horace, who had been present throughout the entire incident and still stood by with one hand against his smarting face.

The next morning Mama called me into her room to inform me that she would be spending the day in bed, since she claimed that the "awful episode" of the previous day had left her "physically and emotionally drained." I was very glad to think that I would not have to bump into her in the hall, and more than prepared to bring her cups of tea whenever she wanted, provided that she left poor Horrie alone.

"One thing before you go, Missy," she called as I was leaving. "Fetch me the Sunday papers. There are some sections I have yet to read. Oh, and a pencil too? There's a good girl."

So I left her with her precious papers, reflecting upon the peculiar fact that, though we never seemed to have any money, Mama could always afford her little luxuries.

After I had done my duties for the morning and seen the children eat a lunch of bread and jam, I put them all to bed for a nap. Mama herself had nodded off about midday and I thought it best to ensure that the house remained quiet. This was the first opportunity

I'd had to open the paintbox that Will had bought for me and to try, at the very least, a little experimentation. With this in mind I crept back into Mama's room and gathered a few sheets of the newspaper that had slipped from her bed. I spread these on the kitchen table, then put the beautiful creamy white watercolor paper on top of them. Once I had poured a glass of water, I was ready to open the box and begin.

I was not disappointed. The brush was as soft as could be, the colors quite wonderful — so much so that I could have sat there dabbling for hours. Indeed, I would have done had I not thought it time to empty the water glass, the contents of which had turned a dirty brown with so much rinsing of my brush. As I reached out to pick the glass up, I noticed that a series of circles had been drawn upon the newspaper beneath it. Oh dear, I thought, I've marked Mama's precious "Personal" column, and I bent forward to read what had been of such interest to her.

There, before my eyes, I saw what really attracted Mama to the papers. It was not the search for a husband. Circled in pencil were three advertisements, each seeking a "good mother" to adopt a child. The suitable applicant would be given a fee — two advertisers offered five pounds, the other twenty — to take the baby away, presumably to a place where the mother would never see it again.

I hardly had time to take in the full implication of what I had seen when I heard a shuffle of feet and Mama was standing behind me. "And what do you think you're doing, Missy?" she demanded.

I was certain that she was referring to the advertisements spread before me, but I was mistaken.

"Where, exactly, did you get the money for that?" With this she reached over my shoulder and gripped the paintbox in one hand, lifting it high out of my reach.

"Will bought it for me," I answered truthfully, closing the telltale paper as I did so. "It was a gift."

"A gift, was it? And a very expensive gift, too, I don't doubt. What? Half a crown, was it?"

"No, Mama. Nothing like that. It was only two shillings, honestly."

"Two shillings, was it? And you expect me to believe that? Get to your feet, girl. You have an explanation to give me."

I did as she said, fearful that she would strike me, but she crossed her arms and, assuming a judgmental stance, insisted that I tell her how and when I had acquired the paints. I did this at once and without apology, as I thought none was needed — but I had reckoned without Mama's twisted logic.

"So," she said, sitting herself down at my place, "even though you knew that we were all but destitute, you still allowed this boy to give you money which you then spent upon yourself?"

"Mama," I protested, "I have already explained that Will bought the paintbox for me as a gift. I had no choice in the matter."

"Aha, but you accepted it all the same, didn't you?"

"Yes, but—"

"Then you are a barefaced liar. You did have a choice — the choice not to accept his gift. Or better yet, to ask him, if he must spend his money, to spend it upon our needy family. Heaven knows, he's seen our circumstances often enough, hasn't he?"

"Mama, I couldn't ask that. It would be rude."

"Rude, would it? I'll show you rude, Missy. I'd say there's a good one-and-sixpence worth of paints left in this box when I trade it at the Ipswich pawnbroker's. Would have been more only for the mess you've managed to make of them. Strangely enough, I was thinking of going there on Wednesday as it was. Now I have another reason." She was about to turn on her heel and leave me when she suddenly spotted the papers. "And while you're cleaning up the mess that you've made here, you can return those newspapers to my room, if you don't mind."

The next morning Horace was so deeply asleep that he was still curled up with his thumb in his mouth when I went into his room to call him for breakfast. "Horrie," I whispered, bending over him so that he would not awake with a start. "Horrie, it's time to get up." For a moment I thought that we had lost him, but when I shook his shoulders he opened his eyes and stared around blearily.

"Horrie," I whispered, holding him to me, "I thought you were never going to wake up."

"I did wake up, Missy," he muttered, stretching, "but I am awful sleepy. Can I stay here some more?"

"He can stay there if he likes," Mama's voice came from the doorway. "I've just found sixpence under my bed. The rest of you might like to go down to Old Dibbs for some fresh cream to put on your porridge. See if he's got a quarter of a pint. Now off you go, the lot of you, and leave Horrie in peace."

When Mama was in one of her good moods, it was foolish to waste time wondering why; the best thing to do was to accept it as a blessing and enjoy it. Such was the case that morning. Without another thought we all scrambled out the front door, thinking of nothing but the prospect of stirring fresh cream into our porridge when we returned.

After breakfast was finished and the dishes cleared away I returned to Horrie's room to change his sheets. Once again I found him fast asleep, although this time he was not curled up as before but lying straight as a board, his hands folded on his little chest, his pretty lips fixed in a smile, almost as if he had deliberately arranged himself to trick me into believing that he was still sleeping.

"Come on, Horrie," I said, bending down to him. "Rise and shine or Mama will be in here after you."

But even with that threat he didn't move. I tried another tack. Tickling would stir him up, I was sure of that, and so I began, starting beneath his arms and moving down to his ribs. Still he did not stir. In fact he remained so still that I began to tire of the game and, grasping him by the shoulders, gave him a good shake.

"Horace," I said in my sternest voice, "this has gone far enough. I warn you, if Mama comes in and this bed hasn't been made, there's going to be trouble, believe me."

It was only when he still didn't move, and the fixed smile on his lips did not alter a bit, that I placed my palm on his forehead, wondering if he had sunk into a fever. But he was quite cool, cold even, and thinking perhaps that he had taken some form of fit, I gently lifted his eyelids. The pupils of his eyes were rolled back into his head. I knew then that Horrie was dead, and dropped down onto the bed beside him.

It was Mama who came and found us. I felt a hand attempt to raise me and, knowing it was hers, clung to the little body harder, crying, "He's gone, Mama. Horrie's gone ..."

"I know, Missy," she said. "There's always bad news in this house. Always bad news." She put her arms around me and lifted me up to sit facing her. "Here," she said, using a sheet to wipe my eyes. "Now don't you cry. He's with the angels already."

"You knew that he was gone?" This sudden realization stunned me and I stopped my sniffling at once. "Mama, how did you know?"

Mama lowered her eyes and the corners of her mouth quivered. "Sarah, dear," she began, "I came in to check on the little darling while you were away. He looked so calm, so peaceful, that I knew at once he had passed beyond human sleep ... that he slept in the arms of his Saviour."

I knew then that Mama was lying. Words such as "dear" and "darling" had never been part of her vocabulary for either Horrie or myself. And as for her references to our Saviour and his angels, such terms only passed her lips when she had "bad news" to convey. I did not resume my weeping but asked, as calmly as I could, "Mama, what are you going to do now?"

Her answer was even more callous than I would have given her credit for. "Well, Missy," she said, "I was planning to go to Ipswich tomorrow, as I mentioned last night, so we should see him buried before then."

I gripped the edge of the bed to prevent myself from striking her. "What do you mean by 'we,' Mama?"

She stood up, her massive shape towering over me. "I mean," she said in a businesslike way, "that since we have no money — for the time being, at least — we will have to bury him ourselves."

My wits were too scattered to form a reply,

and so she continued. "I suggest that we leave him here today and tell the children not to come near him, that he is still sleeping and must not be disturbed. Tonight, when they are all asleep, we can take him out to my garden and put him to rest there. If you follow my reasoning ..."

I felt as though I would be sick there and then, and clamped my hand over my mouth to prevent the possibility. My action was not lost on Mama.

"Oh," she declared, "what a miserable creature you are. It's all right for you to sit dabbling in watercolors, Missy Muck, but when you're asked to take some real responsibility, to get your precious artist's hands dirty, you're suddenly too delicate. Now get up and come with me, and if I hear another peep out of you about this business I promise you will never see that precious paintbox again!"

As I got off the bed to follow her from the room, my foot brushed against a pillow, which I instinctively bent to retrieve. It was Mama's, big and plump. Why was it there, beside Horace's bed? I could think of only one reason — and once again, I felt my breakfast rise in my throat.

Out of respect for the memory of Horace, I will not go into the grisly details of what occurred that night. Suffice it to say that when the children were asleep, I was obliged to carry a lantern into the yard while Mama dug in her garden. I had wrapped Horrie in a sheet and it was Mama herself who carried him out and laid him to rest. Mercifully, she did not once shed a tear. If she had, I do not think I could have borne the hypocrisy.

The next day being Wednesday, Mama took the early train to Ipswich, leaving before the little ones were even awake. This was done so that I might tell them she had taken Horace to the doctor as a means of explaining his absence.

She also took my box of paints — whether out of sheer malice or a genuine intention to sell them, it was too soon to tell.

Nevertheless, I was very pleased to be left with the children, and without her.

At six-fifteen that night I heard Mama's footsteps in the hallway, quickly followed by the clamor of children's voices. Within moments she appeared in the kitchen, surrounded by the little ones, and there in her arms I saw the reason for all the excitement. To my utter disbelief she was carrying a new baby. I was at a loss for words and turned away, partly from disgust that she had brought another child into our house when the one she had buried the night before was hardly cold in the ground, and partly to avoid seeing the new arrival's dear little face, since the last thing I wanted was to grow attached to it.

"Well," Mama demanded in her usual bitter tone, "what's the matter with you, Miss? Don't you want to say hello to baby Charles?"

Even when she spoke I refused to turn to her. "What do you think is the matter with me, Mama?" I asked, valiantly attempting to keep my tone even. "Besides, I have the children's dinner to get ready."

"You needn't bother. I have brought a lovely pie, so whatever you're making will have to keep until tomorrow." And with that, she left the room.

Although there was sufficient pie for us all, I could not bring myself to touch it. Mama, however, did not appear to have such a delicate stomach. She dispatched hers with great gusto, even asking if she might have my serving, seeing as it was "going to waste," as she put it. But the thought of what she had done that day, and indeed the day before, would not leave me. When she asked for a pot of tea to conclude her meal, I was more than willing to oblige so that I might quit her presence.

"Here, Mama," I said, setting it in front of her. "Now, if you don't mind, I'd really like to go to bed. I've had a very busy day with the children."

She aimed a dismissive sniff in my direction as I made my way down the corridor, but I had no intention of going to my bedroom. Not then. Knowing that Mama would be a good ten minutes over her tea, I slipped into her room instead and made a beeline for her handbag. Sure enough, there was an opened envelope inside and, within that, a ten-pound note plus a considerable amount of change. I knew then, for certain, where the new baby had come from. Baby Charles was the one who had been advertised for adoption in the Sunday papers. Mama was the so-called "good mother" who had been granted the privilege of raising him with payment of twenty pounds.

That night I went to my bed with a heavy heart. It was clear to me that some years before — long before I was able to remember — some mother had likewise offered me up for adoption and Mama had taken the bait. I wondered then how much had been handed over for me, and why I had been allowed to live. Was it because I was Mama's first adopted child? Or was it to serve as her slave? And was that to be the only future that I could hope for?

I turned to my dreaming stars in the hope that they might lift my spirits, but their beauty brought me only sadness. What was I to do about this nightmare? What hope had I of ever getting away from this place, even if it were only to notify the police of Mama's schemes? And, what was worse, if ever I did escape, what would happen to the children I had grown up with — those that I thought of as my family: Maggie with her limitless imagination and Ben and Josephine, who were as inseparable as twins? And what of baby Victoria?

With these frightful thoughts in mind I must have drifted into an exhausted sleep, because there before me appeared my lady with the green parasol, her lovely kid boots scented with the soft soil of the swamp, her green parasol open and protective above me as I lay in my miserable bed.

7
QUESTIONS AND ACCUSATIONS

"How's Horrie?" Will wanted to know the next time he was down.

I had been expecting the question and, for the first time in my life, was prepared to lie. Mama had a great deal to do with the response that I gave. "If anyone asks," she had warned me, "say that Horace was so ill that I had him admitted to hospital in Ipswich. That should keep any gossips at bay for a while." So that is how I answered Will. I was lying, but it obviously made him happy since he performed a series of cartwheels right there on the road. I, of course, remained on our side of the fence.

"And is your Mama better?" he asked when he had recovered his equilibrium.

"She is well enough to be back on the trains," I answered, "so I suppose she must be."

"Does that mean you've had a chance to try out your paints, then?"

I had anticipated this question too and, mercifully, this time I could tell the truth. "Yes, and they were wonderful," I replied, but when he went on I was less forthcoming.

"What did you paint? Some wildflowers from the swamp?"

"I've experimented with the colors. But I will do more soon, I promise."

"And Mama hasn't objected to you 'wasting time'?"

"Mama will always object to me doing anything but housework," I admitted, "but I'm getting better at standing up for myself. Besides, I don't really have much extra time. We have a new baby in the house, you know."

Judging by the look of astonishment on his face, I could have knocked him down with a feather. "Another baby? After Victoria?"

"Yes," I answered, trying to pass this off lightly. "His name is Charles. He's lovely."

"Sarah," he said, "these babies, they can't possibly be your Mama's, can they?"

"I never said that they were," I answered curtly.

"So, where do they come from?"

I was trapped, as I had known I would be

sooner or later. This was why Mama had not wanted us to get too close to people. "People are stickybeaks," she had always warned, "and how this family lives is none of their business."

Still, I decided to answer Will honestly. After all, it was not how Mama acquired her children that bothered me so much — I had convinced myself that her "adoptions" must have been legal if they were advertised in the papers. It was how she disposed of them that made me suspicious. So I said, "Do you remember the cuttings that Mama had taken from the Sunday papers? Well, they weren't advertisements by men looking for wives; they were put in by mothers offering their babies for adoption. Mama, loving babies as much as she does, applies as often as she can."

Will's eyes narrowed. "But Sarah," he said, moving closer to the fence as if to share a confidence, "she has too many little ones as it is. Besides, you're always telling me that she has no money."

"Oh, that's not a problem," I answered as off-handedly as I could manage. "The mothers always give Mama something for support."

"Something? What do you mean 'something'?"

"Money. Usually about twenty pounds, so far as I know."

"Twenty pounds? That wouldn't last long."

"She has her sewing," I countered, still attempting to protect her. "She gets money for that too."

But Will said no more on the topic and excused himself, saying that he had to help his Uncle Bertie. As for me, I slowly returned to the house, already fearful that I had divulged too much.

The very next morning, Mama was fussing about in the back garden while I was tidying away the breakfast things when the children came running to inform me that Old Bertie was paying us a visit. Naturally, they thought that he had come to leave a gift for us, but I, more than mindful of what I had told Will the day before, thought that our visitor might have other reasons. What if Will had told him how Mama acquired her babies? What if he asked where they were? How could the absence of Robbie and Horrie be explained away?

I had little time to arrive at answers to these questions before he had entered our gate. He went straight to the front door, where he knocked loudly, and I hurried through the hall to greet him — eager to find out what he wanted and to send him on his way if it was to do with Mama and her babies. But this fear was utterly unfounded. Immediately I opened the door, a bunch of the most beautiful roses was thrust at me and I stepped back, thoroughly confused.

"Miss Pratchett," he declared, "I was expecting your Mama. Is she home, eh?"

"She is in the back garden, Mr. Quaver," I informed him. "If you give me a moment, I'll fetch her for you," and with that, I hurried through the house to find her, satisfied that he would not have come to interrogate her bearing roses.

"It's Mr. Quaver back again," I said, finding her with her bottom up among the turnips. "And this time he's got a bunch of roses."

"Well then, he'll just have to leave them, won't he?" she answered gruffly, not attempting to lift her head, and providing me with the most unpleasant sight of her fat and hairy legs, from her knees to her gardening boots. "I wouldn't be taking callers looking like this, would I?"

"But Mama, he's at the door, and he's been so kind. Please come and see him. He's waiting."

With her face set in a scowl, she wiped her dirty hands on her apron and clumped through the hall. I was afraid at first that she was going to bite his head off, but I should have known her better. By the time she reached the door she had managed to change her scowl into a delightful smile (insofar as Mama could smile delightfully). She greeted our visitor with a highly convincing "Why, Mr. Quaver, these could never be for me?", upon which she plunged her nose into the depths of the bouquet, closed her eyes, and sniffed. "Heavenly," she declared when she had drawn breath. "Just heavenly."

I could barely refrain from stepping forward and saying to the poor man, "Go now! Can't you see that this is all pretense?" But I held my tongue and slipped quietly into my room, intent on listening to what might transpire from beneath my window.

Bertie allowed Mama time to eulogize over the roses, then he cleared his throat and said, "Mrs. Pratchett, you must know that I've been concerned for your welfare for some time, and now the moment has come to discuss how I might best arrange to care for you — and yours — on a permanent basis."

"Oh, Mr. Quaver," I heard Mama reply in a syrupy voice. "You shouldn't, really—"

"No, no," he cut in. "You must not believe this concern is entirely related to your suffering, which I see is acute. I confess to having suffered myself — you see, I have suffered the agonies of the lonely heart."

At this I heard a sort of a scuffle, or at least the rapid movement of bodies, and I raised myself to peer out of my window. There, to my amazement, was Old Bertie on his knees before Mama, her hands gripped tightly in his. I stuffed my knuckles into my mouth to prevent myself from making a noise — either laughing or crying, I cannot be certain — and heard him offer the following plaintive appeal:

"Ah, Mrs. Pratchett, you do not know how you affect me as you pass me by at the station. And when I saw you in that red dress, I knew the time had come to surrender myself to you, the woman I love. The woman I would ask to be my wife, if she would have me?" Here his voice was raised to a pitch that was barely endurable to the human ear, and I suppose that, from our separate vantage points, Mama and I realized at this moment that the wretched man had proposed marriage to her!

I watched wide-eyed, waiting to see Mama's response. For once, she seemed too flabbergasted to reply.

"Mr. Quaver," she muttered after a silence, "I am overcome," as I believe she was. It had been one thing for her willingly to accept the man's gifts, but now that he had finally admitted the true reason for his many kindnesses to her, she realized that she must set the record straight. And since this meant being honest — to both herself and another — it was no easy matter for Mama to resolve — at least not there and then, with a man kneeling before her and a bunch of roses in her hand!

So she continued to "um" and "ah" until she managed to control her thoughts sufficiently to say, "Dear Mr. Quaver, come now, sit here beside me," and from the sound of their footsteps and the sigh of cane stretching, I assumed that she had led him to our weather-beaten cane settee. Now she began to address him in earnest: "It is very flattering to have you come courting, Mr. Quaver," she said, "and an honor which has set my mind reeling, to be sure, but—"

"You are refusing me," I heard him interject. "Ah, but how I hoped. And yet the boy assured me there was no one else."

"The boy?" Mama repeated. "Which boy?"

"My nephew, William, who visits. He has kept me informed of you and yours. And I was foolish enough to believe him."

"What has he informed you of?" Mama demanded, all signs of her previous swooning tones now lost. "I have a high regard for my privacy, you know. The highest regard, Mr. Quaver! I will not stand for anyone gossiping about me. There are certain things—"

"No, no," the poor man remonstrated. "The boy spoke of you only in the most positive terms." Then he added, his voice suddenly querulous, "Why, should he not? Is there someone? Or something? Eh?"

I could just make out Mama's face. If Bertie had wanted to win her heart, he had now lost all hope. The worst thing that anyone could do was question Mama — to her, privacy was all! I saw that she had colored up as red as a tomato, and I would have warned the man had it not entailed revealing my whereabouts.

"Mr. Quaver," she burst out, "unless I am mistaken, this tête-à-tête was intended as a proposal of marriage, but it seems to have become an inquisition — which, as I consider myself a lady, I will terminate forthwith!"

With that declaration I heard Mama begin to stride towards the front door, where I assume she must have turned to him again, since a haughty "Good day!" resounded before the door was slammed upon him.

As for me, I threw myself immediately under my bed, where I lay silent and out of sight until her thunderous footsteps had passed my door.

Well, I thought, at least that puts an end to Old Bertie's chances of becoming my Papa. Then another likelihood arose, one which I had never considered. Given that Bertie had spoken so freely of Will's part in all this, I began to doubt that I would ever see him again, not with Mama's permission, at least, and I covered my head with my hands to stifle my sobbing.

But the Good Lord works in mysterious ways, as I was beginning to learn.

On the following Saturday the children came running to announce that Will was showing a man and a woman to our house — and the man was in uniform, "like a policeman," Ben added, wide-eyed.

On hearing this, my stomach sank. I assumed that Dibbs from the store had turned Mama's long overdue account over to the authorities and now we would suffer the added ignominy of being declared bankrupt in front of our friend. This was the last thing that I wanted the little ones to hear.

Removing my soiled apron, I gathered Maggie and Ben to me and held them close. "Listen carefully, both of you," I whispered. "Mama has some very important business to discuss. Grown-ups' business, you understand? I want you to play in the yard with Will until they're gone. Now, off you go, and take Josephine with you."

"But I want to see the policeman," Ben whined, and before I could silence him Mama herself boomed from the back door, "What policeman, pray tell?"

"They say that there is a policeman headed for the house, Mama. Will Quaver and a woman are coming too."

I saw the color drain from her face and she staggered for a moment, clutching at the door jamb for support, but she recovered just as quickly and hissed, "Get the babies out. And this lot too, do you hear? Go around the back of the house and over the side fence. Take them down to the swamp. Now, do you hear? Get those babies and get out."

I knew that the time had come to stand my ground. I had nothing to be ashamed of, so why should I run? "No, Mama," I said, folding my arms across my chest as a statement of my defiance, "I will not get the babies. And I won't run either, especially into the swamp. I was never allowed to go there when I wanted, so why should I go now that it suits you? Besides, I've already told the children to play in the yard, and that's exactly what they're going to do."

As Mama stood aghast at my sudden exhibition of courage, I shooed the children away with my hands. They needed little encouragement after seeing the fury in Mama's face and, no doubt, predicting the consequences, which I was left to face alone.

"Just what do you think you're doing?" Mama muttered through clenched teeth. "What have you told that boy?" She was moving across the room as she spoke, her hand raised to strike me, but in that instant there was a knock at the front door and, making the most of her momentary hesitation, I scurried around her to run the length of the hallway, crying, "Coming! Coming!" at the top of my voice.

Will stood on the veranda in the company of a middle-aged woman and a police officer in full uniform. "Will?" I said foolishly. "Will?" And then I burst into tears. So much for the duration of my courage!

But Will was quick to rescue me. "Sarah," he said, putting his arm around my shoulder, "this is my mother, Mrs. Emily Quaver, and this is Sergeant Cleeland. They've come all the way from Ipswich just to talk to you."

Before the introductions could be formalized, Mama's voice cut in. "Well, have they now? How nice for them. If they hurry, they will just get to the station in time to catch the ten-twenty train back, because they won't be talking to this little Miss without my permission." And with that, she pulled Will's arm from my shoulder and dragged me bodily towards her, where, struggle as I might, I was no match for the grip of her mighty arms.

"Mrs. Pratchett, I presume?" the sergeant asked, almost too politely. "Or is it Miss Pratchett? I am unclear on that point."

"I am sure you are," Mama replied nastily, "and will remain so, since it's none of your business."

"Oh, but it is my business," he replied, his voice as smooth as silk, "as is the way you are holding that child. I suggest that you release her immediately. You see, she is my witness."

"Witness? Witness?" Mama repeated, her voice rising. "Your witness?"

"Yes, Mrs. Pratchett. Acting on advice that young Will here has passed on to his mother, and which I have checked, I was wondering if you, or young Sarah, could provide us with information on the whereabouts of the boy Horace Pratchett, last seen at this address?"

Upon hearing this, Mama and I stood aghast. I have no idea why she thought these people had come, but this was the worst situation that I could ever have imagined, and realizing the seriousness of it all, I pulled myself from Mama's grip and scampered away to seek the protection of Sergeant Cleeland.

Mama now released a loud "Harumph!", as if to indicate that Horrie's whereabouts was a problem easily solved. "Horace Pratchett was a resident in this house," she began, her tone suddenly sounding assured, "but now, due to illness, he is hospitalized."

"Really? And in what hospital might he be found?"

Mama was silent, apparently contemplating her next move, or possibly attempting to remember the exact contents of the lie that she had forced me to rehearse so carefully. "Again, that is personal and none of your business," she said loftily, but I could see no reason why I shouldn't answer — and truthfully, at that.

"If anybody had asked me that question," I said, peering out from behind the sergeant, "I was told to answer that Horrie was in the Ipswich hospital — and so that's what I told Will when he asked."

"There, you see, Mother," Will whispered, tugging at his mother's skirt. "So Sarah told the truth."

I was about to contradict him, explaining that I had only told a partial truth, when Mrs. Quaver spoke up. "Will has told me so much about you, Mrs. Pratchett. And so has his uncle, my brother-in-law Mr. Bertram Quaver, the station master. Bertie writes to me almost weekly, the dear man. When little Horace became ill, I felt sorry for you — missing the child as you must, and he you. So I went to visit him in the hospital. I even bought some lovely oranges for him. But they told me he wasn't there. That he'd never been there. Nor had they ever heard of you. And when Will told me the remainder of Sarah's story—"

"What story? What has she been saying? Tell me ..."

Mrs. Quaver continued, unperturbed. "—I took it upon myself to speak with Sergeant Cleeland here. It appears that he found the whole thing even more frightening than I did."

"Frightening? Frightening?" The haughtiness had quite vanished from Mama's tone. Instead, she had assumed the manner of the long-suffering mother. "Yes, 'frightening' is a word to describe my sorry life. Here I am, alone in the world with only the company of my little ones to keep my heart alive, to give me the love that every mother craves. And what do I receive in return? Lies and rumors, no doubt spread by the likes of your son here, and that miserable man, your brother-in-law, Quaver, who came dancing attention on me. Yes, I have even suffered the betrayal of those I have nursed since they were babes. Those who would never have had a roof over their heads or a crust of bread in their stomachs. Even those whose own mothers abandoned them ..." During this speech Mama had lifted her crumpled apron to her eyes in an attempt to feign weeping, but she paused a moment to glare at me.

"That is all very well," the sergeant said, reaching out to touch her arm, and for an instant I feared that he might have been fooled by her tent-show theatrics, "but you still have not answered my question, which is not, by the way, a personal one. The whereabouts of Horace Pratchett is my business, as is the disappearance of any person, whether one of your children or otherwise."

"Well," said Mama matter-of-factly, "if Horace is not in the Ipswich hospital, which is where I left him, I have no idea where he might be. It would appear, Sergeant, that it should be me who is asking you to find him, not vice versa. It seems to me, as his mother, that there is a kidnapper on the loose!"

"If that is so, Mrs. Pratchett, how do you account for the fact that no one at the hospital has a record of the child's admission?"

"I rushed him in there late one night. It is quite possible, since his admission was an emergency, that such formalities were overlooked."

"Rushed him in at night, you say?"

"Well, the early hours of the morning. Between 2 and 3 a.m., I should think."

"Was that on a weekday?" Will piped up.

"Will," his mother remonstrated, "be quiet!"

But the sergeant turned to the boy. "Why, son?"

"Uncle Bertie told me he closes the station down at 10 p.m. on weekdays because there aren't enough passengers in or out of Waterford for it to stop. There's not another train until 5 a.m. Even on weekends there are no trains running after 11. I know that, because it's the latest I can go home. If I'm up late playing chess with Uncle Bertie, that is."

Now the sergeant turned slowly towards Mama, his eyebrows raised. "So, Mrs. Pratchett, how did you get to Ipswich if it wasn't by train?"

"I never said a word about trains," Mama shouted. "It was that brat there who was talking about trains. Why, Horrie was so sick and I was

119

so worried that I lost all reason, as a mother does when her baby's at death's door. I just gathered him up and ran. I wasn't even sure where I was going. All I wanted to do was find help, and as I ran, a sulky that was passing pulled over and a kindly gentleman asked if he could help. I couldn't tell you his name, but that's how I got to Ipswich."

I had noticed that Mama's tone had grown more and more confident as this masterpiece of fiction poured from her lips. Worse, it seemed that the sergeant was finally about to admit defeat in the face of her evidence — even though it was unverifiable.

"Then it seems, Mrs. Pratchett, that I will have to do a little more spadework before we meet again. We will meet again, I am certain of that. Thank you for your time."

He was in the process of tipping his cap to Mama when I shocked even myself by clutching his coattail and crying, "Wait!"

"What now, little Miss?" he asked kindly, turning to me.

"You can't leave me here. Not now," I cried, refusing to let go of him. "She will get me, she will, I know it."

"Get you? What do you mean, 'get you'?"

"She will beat me, that's what she will do.

For talking to Will. For telling him things about her. About all of us."

"Mrs. Pratchett," the sergeant asked Mama directly, "is this true?"

Mama smiled and managed to reach out to stroke my head. "Why, Sergeant, Sarah is my right hand. I don't know what I would do without her. Beat her? Heavens above, I'd just as soon put my arm in boiling water. Come now, Missy, let the sergeant go or he'll miss his train, there's a dear," and she reached out again, this time a good deal more deliberately. I ducked to avoid her, but as I did I saw the look in her eyes. I have never seen such menace, such hatred, and I knew then for a certainty that if I was left with her I should be her next victim.

Driven by this fear, I released my hold on the sergeant's jacket and ran to the other side of the veranda. With only the swamp behind me — to which I could escape if necessary — I gripped the veranda rail with one hand and pointed the other accusingly at Mama. "Don't believe a word of what she has told you. She is a liar," I managed to blurt out, "and a wicked, wicked woman. A murderess! Yes! A murderess!"

"That is quite an accusation, Miss," the sergeant said, his voice as calm as could be. "It is no wonder that you should expect a beating if you accuse your mother of that."

Now I knew that I must defend myself or die. "Dig up our back garden, then," I answered, "but please, please, don't leave me here with her."

8

MAMA'S LOST LAMBS

I did not have to spend that day with Mama, nor did the children. Uncle Bertie, although he was shocked to see Mama taken away, provided an abandoned railway carriage, which Will and Maggie very quickly transformed into the most wonderful nursery. It was also thanks to Bertie's telegraph that Sergeant Cleeland was able to call down reinforcements so quickly. Much to the children's delight — especially Ben's — three troopers' horses were soon tied to our front fence, although the little ones had no inkling why the men had come. I wish that I could say the same.

When the children had been settled in their carriage by the station I was led to the rear of our house and asked to indicate the where-abouts of Horrie's body. Mama had planted a pumpkin vine in the garden since the time of his death, but this was not my only reason for appearing suddenly vague. I was fearful of the horror that I had unveiled and began to realize that there was no turning back.

Still, I did my best to inform Sergeant Cleeland of where I thought the body had been buried, then he, in turn, instructed his troopers, who dutifully removed their trenching shovels from the horses and began to dig. The day wore on with little success and I grew more and more afraid. Had all of this been no more than a waking nightmare? After all, I reminded myself, I had seen the vision of the lovely woman by daylight, a circumstance which I dared not reveal to anyone but Will, for fear of being judged mad. And yet, acting on my word, here in my own backyard was a company of troopers digging up my mother's garden in search of a child's body.

By two o'clock, when nothing had been found, Mrs. Quaver went into the kitchen with me to make tea for the troopers. They had already gone without a midday meal, such was the importance that the sergeant attached to the search.

"Are you all right?" Mrs. Quaver asked as I busied myself with the familiar task of boiling the kettle. "You know that you can talk to me, if you would like."

"I don't know what to think," I admitted. "I want to pray to God that this will all be over soon, but for that to happen they will have to find Horrie's body. I mean, I'm certain that it's there, I saw Mama bury him, but I can't stop wishing that it wasn't. Don't you see?"

Mrs. Quaver left off setting out our chipped and tea-stained cups and crossed the room to hug me. I was sure that she was a good woman. It must have taken great strength for her to present her case to Sergeant Cleeland. Nor would every mother have sufficient faith in her son to stake her good standing in the community on such a seemingly far-fetched tale. But Mrs. Quaver had. When she stooped to draw me to her, how I wished that I had a mother just the same.

That, I now realized, was never to be, since even the surrogate mother I had once had was now lost to me. Or at least she would be if they found the evidence of her terrible handiwork.

Not long after three o'clock the call went up that a body had been found. I admit I sighed with relief. The troopers congregated in a huddle, and after some whispered discussion Sergeant Cleeland came striding towards me. I thought that he was coming to comfort me and tell me that the worst was over. In this I was wrong.

"Sarah," he said, kneeling on the grass beside me, "exactly how old was Horace?"

In the circumstances, I thought this a very strange question. "I don't know for certain," I said. "Mama had birthdays that we kept each year, but now that I understand we were all adopted, I couldn't really say for certain."

"No, no," he smiled reassuringly. "I don't want the day and the month, but was he closer to two than three, would you say?"

"Closer to three. He was too advanced to be much younger."

"Advanced? How do you mean, 'advanced'?"

"He was tall. Mama always said that if he kept on growing he would be able to get a job as a giant in a circus."

At this the sergeant was silent for some time, and I could tell that he was wrestling with a problem.

"What is it?" I queried. "Haven't you found him?"

"Perhaps what we have found is worse," he muttered, partly to himself. Then, as if firming in his resolve, he lifted his head and asked directly, "Sarah, did your Mama ever tell you that any other children in the family had been admitted to hospital, or even died, lately?"

How could I possibly forget? "Little Robbie,"

I answered at once, but even as the name left my lips I understood the reason for the sergeant's question.

"Then there must be two," I heard him say, and leaving me to the comfort of Mrs. Quaver, he returned to his men.

9
THE TRUTH
ABOUT MAMA

Upon the discovery of the bodies in our
garden, Sergeant Cleeland took Mama into
custody at the Ipswich Police Station, where
she was formally charged with murder.

The children knew nothing of this. They
were simply told that their Mama would be
away for a while. I doubt that any of them really
missed her, since we were all given into the care
of Mr. and Mrs. Quaver, which meant that we
could be with Will every day. As for the two
babies, Victoria and Charles, the police were
able to track down their real mothers. Having
heard the circumstances under which Mama
was being detained, I doubted that they would
willingly advertise their children for "adoption"
again.

Three long weeks passed before Mama could
be brought to trial. This was a strange time for

me. On the one hand I loved being with the Quavers, especially Will, but on the other I still had no idea what my future held or what lay in store for the other children. If Mama was found innocent, there was a chance that we would be returned to her; if guilty, we would be farmed out to someone else — the Quavers could not keep us all indefinitely. So, while my days were filled with good company, at night I longed for my old room with its starry view — although "my lady of the swamp" still came walking in my dreams, and her presence cheered me a great deal.

At last the day of Mama's trial came. Mrs. Quaver had outfitted me with new clothes and I attended the courtroom with her and Will, since all three of us had been called as witnesses.

I entered the court with a sense of dread, gripping Mrs. Quaver's hand and keeping my eyes cast down. It was three weeks since I had seen Mama and I was afraid that if I looked up, I would be caught by her withering gaze. Even when the judge entered, I stood without raising my head, but I knew that sooner or later I must find the courage to look Mama in the eye.

I waited until His Honor announced that the court was in session and Sergeant Cleeland had been called as the first witness. Then, believing that Mama would be concentrating upon him, I slowly raised my eyes.

I was foolish to do so. Although the sergeant testified against Mama in terms that would have reduced anyone else to tears, she still found the strength to look down upon me from the dock as if I were a piece of carrion thrown before a vulture. I was made to feel that if she could, she would have swooped down and torn me to pieces. One glance was enough to convince me that she placed the blame for all that had happened upon my shoulders and thought it was I who should be on trial for being an ungrateful daughter — a charge that she doubtless considered worse than murder.

I averted my gaze and tried to concentrate on what the sergeant was saying. It seemed that he was giving an account of what had happened on the fateful day Mrs. Quaver and Will had brought him to our house. When his testimony had drawn to a close, I expected that Mama's defense lawyer would cross-examine him — at least that was what Mrs. Quaver had led me to expect — but in this I was wrong. The prosecutor, a man called Mr. Oxley, chose to open a new line of questioning and the sergeant was only too willing to oblige.

"Sergeant Cleeland," Oxley began, gathering a set of papers and adjusting his wig before approaching the witness box, "I understand that there is further evidence that you wish to submit to the court, relevant to the charges that have been laid against the accused, Mrs. Agnes Pratchett. Is that so?"

In different circumstances I might have giggled to hear Mama's Christian name spoken out loud.

"Yes, there is other evidence," the sergeant answered.

"Please proceed," Oxley directed him, "and take your time."

I will not elaborate upon all that the sergeant disclosed that day, but suffice it to say he had certainly done his "spadework" carefully. Every residence that Mama had lived in for the past decade was listed, as well as the duration of her stay there. I remembered some of them, but many I did not. I was stunned by how short Mama's stay in each had been. I was able to calculate that two or three months had been her usual tenancy up until Maggie arrived.

"And have you subsequently investigated these addresses, Sergeant?" the prosecutor inquired, although he knew the answer already, I guessed.

"Yes," Sergeant Cleeland answered. "I had a search warrant prepared for each."

"What exactly were you looking for?" the judge asked, his brow furrowed as he leaned across his bench. "Not more bodies, I trust?"

"Yes, Your Honor."

"And did you find any?"

At this the sergeant lowered his head as if he were taking a long, slow breath. Never had I experienced such a sustained silence. Not a person coughed, not a chair scraped — all were hanging on his answer. At last he looked up and spoke, his voice low, each word measured. "In company with my troopers, I had the misfortune to witness the unearthing of eight more bodies from the yards or gardens of those addresses once occupied by the accused. Or, more accurately, eight skeletons — all of children aged between two and five years, I am sorry to say."

"And the cause of death?" the prosecutor asked.

"Unknown," came the answer, but before this reply could fully register, a shout of "Why not say 'natural causes'?" rang through the court. Everyone's attention was drawn to Mama, who had risen in her box.

"Answer me, man," she continued. "Why not

say 'natural causes' instead of 'unknown'? Or are you afraid that all your snooping will prove to be no more than a waste of time?"

"Order! Order in the court," the judge commanded, bringing down his gavel. "I warn you, Ma'am, that you can be charged with contempt of court."

Upon hearing this, Mama slumped back into her seat with a sneer, but her point was not lost upon her defense lawyer, Slater, who opened his questioning with the very same argument. "And so you have been able to find no evidence at all that these children were murdered, Sergeant? Is that what we are to believe?"

Sergeant Cleeland appeared momentarily unsettled. He inserted a finger in his collar and stretched it before answering. "That is correct, but—"

"No, no," Slater interrupted. "There can be no 'ifs' or 'buts' in the law. Surely you know that."

Now the sergeant rallied. He lifted his head and confidently replied, "I was not attempting to cover some incompetence on my part, Sir. I merely wished to make the point that there could be no explanation other than death by violence. The odds are against anything—"

But again the defense cut him short. "Really,

Sergeant," he chuckled, "you would not have this trial won or lost on the basis of 'odds,' would you? Why, Mrs. Pratchett does not look like a racehorse to me."

At this the court broke into laughter and the judge banged his gavel again. Even Mama smirked, and I wondered if indeed she might win, and shuddered at the thought.

So the day proceeded, and the next too, with Mama's defense seeming to claim a point or two while Mr. Oxley, the prosecutor, did the same. But on the second day, after lunch recess, Will was called to the stand, where he explained clearly how he had been alerted to the troubles in our home. So confident was he that Mama finally took her eyes off me and turned her stare upon him, no doubt regarding him as a traitor as well.

When Mrs. Quaver was called, she said Will had reported that Mama was bringing home babies advertised for adoption in the newspapers — and how others had inexplicably vanished. She told of the use that Mama had made of "Mother Hibberd's Soothing Syrup — the Mother's Friend" and how she had learned that its basic ingredient was laudanum, a drug which could prove fatal to a small child.

Mr. Oxley next called the chief physician of

the Ipswich hospital to verify Mrs. Quaver's opinion with scientific evidence, and I saw the judge and certain members of the jury take notes of what he said.

When the doctor had stepped down from the witness box, I heard the bailiff call my name and knew that my time of testing had come. Despite all that the court had heard from others, I was the only one who had lived with Mama, a circumstance which placed me in the unenviable position of being the prosecution's "principal witness."

As I stood up, Mrs. Quaver squeezed my hand and Will gave me a wink. It was good to know that, whatever happened, they would be there when I was finished. I crossed the courtroom without looking at Mama and climbed into the witness box. When I was settled and the bailiff was approaching me with the bible to swear upon, the judge suddenly raised his hand.

"Just a moment," he said. "Miss Pratchett, as you are a minor, I have the option of asking an adult to corroborate your evidence rather than having you take the oath. But since I can think of no adult who has been privy to your lives together other than the accused herself, that would be impossible. For this reason, before you take the oath, I must make something very clear to you." Here he paused and crossed his arms on the bench. "Sarah, I should bring to your attention that you need not proceed if you do not wish to. Although you were not legally adopted by the accused, Mrs. Pratchett, to all intents and purposes she has raised you as her daughter. In fact it is probably fair to say that you have known no other mother. Is that true?"

I could not seem to find my voice, so I nodded in agreement.

"In that case, I think that you should know that I cannot order you to take the stand against this woman. Is that clear?"

"Yes, Your Honor," I answered, although my voice had a shrill, nervous tone that I hated.

"Then I ask you, Sarah, do you still wish to proceed as a witness, given that you may be asked to testify against your mother, so-called?"

As long as I live I hope that I will never again be asked to answer such a question. Mama's life depended on my decision, as did my own peace of mind and future well-being. But answer the judge I must, and in such a way that my conscience would be forever clear. So I took one deep breath and said, "Yes, Your Honor. I do wish to testify," and having said that, I knew that I would come through.

"State your full name to the court," the bailiff said before I could gather my wits, and at once I was plunged into confusion.

"I don't know my full name," I answered truthfully. "I am called Sarah Pratchett, but as you know—"

"Sarah Pratchett will do for our purposes," the judge said, "unless the accused could offer the court the child's true surname?"

I did not want to face Mama, but I heard her "Harumph" from the dock and assumed that she had declined to answer. The next moment, as I lifted my head and prepared to place my hand upon the bible before me, I saw — or thought I saw — my lady of the swamp seated in the body of the court. It was such a fleeting glimpse that I later believed I had imagined it, although at the time no woman could have appeared more real.

When the questioning started, I stood as tall as I could and held my chin high. It felt good to know that I was wearing a brand new store-bought dress and new stockings and boots. Mrs. Quaver had also used her crimping irons to wave my usually thin, lank hair, so I knew that I should not feel ashamed of my appearance — nor indeed of the truth that I was about to tell.

Mr. Oxley, the prosecutor, was very kind to me, helping me to express myself more clearly by rephrasing his questions so that I could better understand, but generally he asked me simply to tell what I had seen happening at home, both before and after the arrival of a new child. And of course I could only agree when he suggested that there was a connection between a new arrival and a sudden departure. Nor could I deny that such arrivals were usually babies, while the departures were usually toddlers.

"And why do you think that might have been, Sarah?"

I was about to answer when a roar like that of a bull almost caused me to fall from the stand. "Objection! Objection, Your Honor!" Mama's defense lawyer, Slater, was bellowing. "How can a child possibly comment on the workings of an adult mind? It is preposterous to imagine that this ... this girl could understand—"

But the judge brought down his gavel hard, demanding silence. "Objection overruled," he announced. "From my understanding of this case to date, we have among us one of the very few children who is capable of understanding the adult mind. Heaven help her, she has experienced little enough of childhood!"

Mr. Slater returned to his seat red-faced.

"To repeat my question," Oxley said, "why do you think that when your Mama collected a new baby, an older child — a toddler, let us say often disappeared?"

"I can think of several reasons," I answered.

"Yes ..." he encouraged.

"Well, one is that Mama loves babies. She doesn't like children much. Especially noisy boys."

"And Robbie and Horace were noisy boys?"

"Horrie was. Yes. He was always 'full of beans,' as Mama would say."

"And it is a matter of record that Horace died immediately before the new baby, Charles, arrived?"

"That's true. The day before."

"And there were other reasons why you believed that this pattern of appearance and disappearance occurred?"

"The older the babies grew, the more money Mama needed to support them."

"And your Mama would get ten or twenty pounds in cash when she 'adopted' a new baby? Is that true?"

"After she brought home Victoria and Charles, I found banknotes in her handbag."

"Thief!" Mama screamed. "How can you

believe a thief? Ask her where she got the money for her paintbox. Ask her. Go on. I demand that you ask her!"

"You, Ma'am, are in no position to demand anything," the judge reminded her. "I will not hesitate to have you forcibly removed from the court, should you interrupt proceedings again."

And so my time in the witness box dragged on. Ever aware that I was betraying Mama, I knew that I must tell the truth if I was to protect other children from a terrible fate.

When at last Mr. Oxley had finished with me, Mr. Slater rose to cross-examine. I admit that I was already intimidated by this man's behavior. I did not think for a minute that he was sorry for me, and now that he had me all to himself, I was fully aware that his principal intention — in fact his role in the trial — was to discredit my testimony so that Mama might go free.

As soon as he began, my worst fears were confirmed.

"Sarah," he said, "do you love your Mama?"

"Sometimes I do," I answered truthfully.

"And when do you not love her?"

"When she does things like call me a thief, as she did before."

"And are you a thief, Sarah? Did you, as your Mama suggested, take money from her purse?"

"I have never stolen from Mama. The paint-box that she spoke of was a gift to me from Will Quaver. He is here, in the court. You can ask him if you doubt my word."

"And that was the only time you did not love her? When she called you names?"

"No. I did not love her when she forced me to do things that were not right."

"Come, come. What mother would force her daughter to do things that were not right?"

"She forced me to give the sleeping syrup to Horace. I told her that it was doing him no good and that it could be harmful, but she ignored me. And later, she made me help her bury him. I don't think those things were right and I didn't love her then."

Upon hearing this, he put a finger to his chin, as if thinking deeply, and held this pose for so long that the judge finally said, "We are waiting, Mr. Slater," upon which he addressed me again.

"I must apologize, Sarah, for keeping you so long. You see, the implications of your answer were so significant that I needed time to ruminate upon them." He spoke with such an oily voice that I might have poured it onto a spoon and swallowed it as an emetic. "Now, let us proceed. From what we have just heard, you were not pleased with your mother — no, I will rephrase that. From what you have just told us, it is clear that you did not love your mother during the time immediately before the death of the child, Horace — and certainly not immediately after it."

I suspected that the man was trying to trick me, but what he had said was a fair summary of my answer, and true enough, so I accepted it and agreed.

"Now then, Sarah, it would be reasonable to say that 'not loving' your mother meant that you did, in fact, despise her, wouldn't it?"

"Objection, Your Honor," Mr. Oxley cried. "The defense is leading the witness."

"Sustained," the judge announced. "You will rephrase the question, Mr. Slater."

"Very well, Your Honor. Sarah, about the time we were discussing, what were your feelings towards your mother?"

"I was angry with her."

"Were you also angry with her because she would not let you go out?"

I was more and more certain that I was being led to make an admission that I would later regret, but Mr. Slater was so skilled in his questioning and I was so tired that I could do little to prevent him. "Yes, I was a bit angry about that. But—"

"Were you especially angry because your Mama, who had always been very protective of you, would not let you go out with the boy, Will Quaver?"

Now I began to understand where he was leading me. I also detected the hand of Mama in the framing of his questions. This particular piece of malice must have come directly from her.

"There were times—" I said, attempting a response, but Mr. Slater was fast and sharp, and before I could finish he made the statement which drove his point home.

"So then, Miss Sarah" — when he called me this I knew for certain that he was Mama's minion — "it would be reasonable to say that you had a number of reasons to tell the police and this court that you found your mother's pillow beside the deathbed of the boy, Horace, would it not?"

"But I did," I protested.

He was still too quick for me. "You told the court a lie, that's what you did. You told a lie because you hated your mother for not letting you run the streets with the first boy who came along. To be rid of her, you have tried to convince us that she is a murderess. That she first attempted to murder her child with cough syrup overdoses, and when this failed she smothered him with her own pillow. Would you have the court believe that this woman, who loved children so much that she would take in those whose own mothers rejected them, is a murderess? Come now. Look at her. Please, look at your mother. I put it to the jury, is this not the face of every mother — of every woman who has known the suffering of a mother?"

Of all the professions that Mama might have undertaken, I would never have considered her capable of acting, but judging by the performance which followed, she rated among the Ellen Terrys and Sarah Bernhardts of the stage. She did not cry outright — not in great sobs and gulps — oh no. Rather, she wept silently, as if her grief sprang from wells of emotion too deep for all but a mother's heart. As her finale, she turned towards me and cried, once, "Sarah, my first. My baby ..." then dropped her head into her hands and refused to lift it, despite offers of comfort from Mr. Slater and demands for order from the judge — although he seemed as convinced of her sincerity as was the remainder of the court.

When my cross-examination was completed, I stepped down from the box exhausted, and both lawyers presented their final summations for the jury. Listening from the body of the court, it seemed to me that the defense had the better case, and I grew more and more certain that Mama would go free. After all, where was the real evidence against her?

Even if the bodies of two hundred children were dug up in Mama's backyard, it did not prove that she had murdered them. And what did my seeing Mama's pillow on the floor beside Horrie's bed have to do with anything? It could have been that one of the little ones left it there after a pillow fight! But accept it as evidence or not, the odds against a single woman who ran an adoption agency having ten of her sixteen originally healthy adoptees die in their first two to four years were very high — unless, of course, their deaths were assisted.

At last the judge directed the jury to retire and consider its verdict. I watched as Mama stepped down from her box and saw a guard pull her arms behind her in order to clamp her wrists with iron manacles. She did not struggle, but allowed herself to be taken away without so much as a backward glance.

Only then did I begin to understand the meaning of pity.

The jury sat for two days considering Mama's case. I know that I could think of little else during that time, so I can't begin to imagine what the state of her nerves must have been.

As the jury filed back into the courtroom I watched Mama's face, but I could read nothing. I can only suppose that, having realized there was little she could do, she was prepared to accept whatever fate had decreed for her.

"Members of the jury," the judge said when all were settled, "have you reached a verdict?"

"We have, Your Honor," the chief juror answered.

"Do you find the prisoner guilty or not guilty of the murder of Horace Pratchett?"

Without batting an eyelid, the juror announced, "We find the accused guilty as charged, Your Honor."

There was no uproar in the court, no fuss or bother, yet I felt my head spin and my body grow limp, as if I were about to faint. No matter what happened now, I knew that I was beyond Mama's influence, for better or for worse, although I could not conceive of anything worse than I had already experienced, especially in those last few months.

But now, I knew, the judge must pass sentence upon Mama, and I attempted to focus my thoughts upon that rather than my own future.

"Mrs. Pratchett," he began, "you have been found guilty of the most serious crime known to humanity: the crime of murder. Although there can be no further superlatives applied to something already defined as the 'most serious,' if there were, then such superlatives would apply to your crime.

"To take the life of a child who has no means of self-defense is the epitome of cowardice; to drug that child before taking its life, as you did, is beyond belief.

"As a result, by the power invested in me by the Crown ..." Here he reached out his hand. I saw at once that he was removing something from beneath the gavel and then, to my horror, I understood. He held a black cap: the sign that Mama was to die.

Without a thought for where I was, I leapt to my feet and cried, "No! She is my mother—" but Mrs. Quaver pulled me down as the judge placed the cap on his head, while his voice continued in steady monotone.

"Agnes Pratchett, the judgment of this court is that you are to be taken from this court and, in the manner and at a time appointed, be hanged by the neck until dead. May God have mercy on your soul."

I have no knowledge of how Mama received

this sentence, as the next thing I remember is regaining consciousness on the settee in the parlor of the Quavers' house. I saw Will's broad smile and his electric red hair. I suppose I knew, even then, that while we were together everything would be all right.

But regarding Mama and her fate, I could think of nothing that made me feel any better. Then, one Sunday, Mrs. Quaver took me to her church. The lesson that the pastor based his sermon upon was, "As ye reap, so shall ye sow." I am sure that he did not prepare this especially for me, but I took it to my heart all the same. It made me feel a little better about what happened to Mama, both then and now.

10

THE ANSWER
OF THE STARS

As I had predicted, the Quavers soon set about finding new homes for the little ones. It was interesting to see that Mama's own explanation for "missing persons" was employed to justify this change of parenthood. Every child was led to believe that Mama was ill and therefore a new Mama — and even a Papa — had to be found for them. Maggie didn't mind this one bit. I had known for some time that her imagination would never have flourished under Mama's strict dictatorship. Thanks to the intelligence and sensitivity of Mrs. Quaver, little Maggie was adopted by a family of potters. They were Bohemians, always traveling about and setting up stalls to sell their wares. I know that Maggie loved them, too, seeing she was allowed to be up to her elbows in clay or paint. That was my Maggie. They were the perfect parents for her, I'm certain. Ben and Josephine were kept together, being adopted as brother and sister. I don't think that I could have borne to see them separated. Once they were gone, there was only me.

One morning when Will was away on an errand, Mrs. Quaver sat me down at the kitchen table and, over a cup of tea, asked me what I would like to do about my future.

"Go to school," I answered immediately. This had been impossible even to consider before the trial, but now that it was over I saw no reason why I shouldn't be like other children.

"That is taken for granted," Mrs. Quaver answered. "But I meant where you live. Most importantly, who will be your family. You should know from the outset, though, that we would love to have you here, if you want to stay. But, after all that you have been through, you need to know that you have a choice."

"If you will have me, there is no choice to make," I told her. "You have been so wonderful to me, and the thought of having Will as both my friend and my brother is more than I could ever have imagined. Thank you. Thank you." And I fell upon her neck and covered her with hugs and kisses.

Life can be very strange. Just when a person

thinks that everything is working out wonderfully, it seems that the whole scheme of things can suddenly change — so that what was wonderful becomes even better. Or perhaps this only applies to those who have appealed to the stars.

Just how could things have worked out better for me? In itself, that is a story which is difficult to believe, but I will do my best to tell it without having it sound like a fairy tale.

One Saturday morning I was lying on the carpet in the Quavers' parlor, reading the papers with Will, when there came a knock at the door. As I had long since given up being the maid, Will went to open it. I took little notice, assuming the visitor was one of Will's school friends come to play, or perhaps one of the charity volunteers with whom Mrs. Quaver worked so closely. Sure enough, Will called from the foot of the stairs, "Mother, there's someone here to see you."

"Show them into the parlor, then," she called back. "I won't be a moment."

I was so deeply involved in the Saturday funnies that I barely lifted my head as the person entered the room and, apart from being vaguely aware of the swish of a skirt, I could not have shown less interest. But as I read on — rudely, I know — and it became necessary to turn a page,

I caught sight of a woman's boot — the most delicate thing and made of finest kid, I was sure. As I noted this, the strangest sensation came over me, and immediately I rose on my elbows to see exactly who was sitting upon the settee.

There was my apparition: my lady of the swamp. It was she in every detail: her dress was of the same butter-colored muslin, her parasol of deep green was folded upon her knees — even her sensible straw hat was the same, right down to the last detail of the gauze veil, which was still mysteriously drawn.

I knew that it was impolite to stare, but I could tell that she was looking down at me, even though her eyes were hidden beneath the veil. I must have worn a perplexed expression upon my face, since she smiled a little and said, "Don't you like the funny pages?"

"Oh yes," I said. "They're the best part of every newspaper, don't you think?"

"The least worrying, certainly," she answered, smiling again, and this time I felt brave enough to take in the pretty shape of her mouth and the fineness of her chin.

I glanced down at my paper for a moment and then, casting caution to the winds, I looked up and said to her, "Please don't think that I'm being impertinent, but haven't we met before?"

"Perhaps," she said, so softly as to be a whisper, but then Mrs. Quaver entered the room and she stood to greet her, saying no more to me.

Mrs. Quaver held out her hand in greeting. "I am Veronica Quaver. How can I help you?"

"Lady Charlotte Islington," our visitor replied, lifting her veil to reveal eyes as green as emeralds. "I have come here on a matter of some confidentiality. Would you prefer that we spoke in private?"

Both Will and I knew the answer to that. As opposed to the thousand and one secrets that Mama had kept to herself, everything in the Quaver household was open to all — which was, I suppose, how Will had come to tell his mother about me in the first place. Mrs. Quaver duly informed Lady Islington of this circumstance, which she accepted more than willingly. "It is good to meet a family with such modern values," she said, and I liked her at once.

"So," Mrs. Quaver inquired, taking a seat and inviting her guest to resume hers, "how can I help you?"

"I do not want to reopen fresh wounds," Lady Islington began, "but if you will allow me briefly to mention one or two recent events, I will be better able to repair the damage of the past."

"Go on," Mrs. Quaver encouraged, though I am certain that Lady Islington's preamble had made as much sense to her as the theory of Newtonian physics.

"I am here because the recently executed murderess, Agnes Pratchett, was once an employee of mine. Having seen her photograph in the papers, and having briefly attended her trial, I was able to trace you."

If she had told us that she had come to call Mama up from her grave, I doubt that she could have shocked us more. But at least what she said proved that I had seen her at the trial — and possibly before, though I chose not to mention that!

"Might I explain?" she asked politely, and so she began. "Some twelve years ago my husband, Sir Julian Islington, and I were engaged in botanical studies in Egypt. That in itself may seem rather odd, but Julian was a brilliant science graduate and had chosen to devote his life to the study of certain herbs found only in the Sahara. He believed that he might extract from them a drug which could cure consumption, or tuberculosis as it is sometimes called. I was fortunate enough to travel with him wherever he went. I am an artist, you see, specializing in botanical subjects, particularly flora."

"You paint flowers?" I blurted out, unable to contain myself.

"Yes," she said, looking down at me. "It was my responsibility to keep a visual record of every plant that Julian studied. It was far too hot to carry cumbersome photographic equipment into the desert. And what would we have done for color? The camera may be a wonderful invention, but it does have its limitations, you see."

"I am learning to draw flowers myself," I told her, "though I'm not very good at it yet."

Lady Islington smiled. "When I finish my tale," she said, "we might discuss our mutual interests further. Now, where was I? In the desert with Julian ... Well, such was our life together. We were ideally suited, Julian and I. And when I learned that I was having a child, we were overjoyed. But the desert is no place for a baby, and since Julian was far from finishing his research, I returned home alone."

"Dear, dear," Mrs. Quaver offered, "you were a very brave woman."

"No, not really, Mrs. Quaver. Neither Julian nor I had a family of our own, so I was quite used to solitude, and besides, shortly after I arrived I gave birth to a dear little girl. But to manage a baby by myself proved very difficult, and so I advertised for a nanny to serve as my companion and to help with the baby. Oh, I interviewed so many bright and charming women and girls, but the one who impressed me most was a woman called Agnes Pratchett."

"Mama!" I declared, and immediately felt stupid for stating the obvious.

"Yes, I believe that she was known as your Mama, and what a strong-willed and practical woman she proved to be. It was not long before I learned to rely on her and trust her implicitly — which was, I suppose, the beginning of the pain which I have been forced to endure over these last, long years." Here she paused to remove a lace handkerchief from her purse and wiped her eyes. I could not help comparing her actions with those of Mama under similar circumstances, but here there was no theatrical affectation.

"Now, now," Mrs. Quaver sympathized. "If you are distressed, Lady Islington, I will make tea. Really, it will help."

"No," she replied. "It is better that I go on. I fear that if I do not have this issue out, I shall never have the opportunity — or the courage — to address it again."

"Yes, yes, dear. Quite," Mrs. Quaver said, although, like Will and myself, she could have no idea what Lady Islington was talking about.

"When the baby had just had her first birthday, Julian asked if I could rejoin him for a month," she continued. "He longed to finish his work and return, but could not do so without my help. I confess that I was devastated at the thought of leaving my darling little one behind, but I could not take such a tiny thing to the desert, and besides, I did so long for Julian to come home. I had no doubt that I could leave the baby in Agnes Pratchett's care, since she had proved so faithful and devoted to the child; but that was the greatest mistake of my life. You see, Julian did not return. In those last weeks of his research he caught fever, there in the desert, and I lost him. How I mourned, alone as I was in that far-off, strange land ... but Julian was not my only loss. Upon my return, I found my house empty. Not only was every piece of furniture missing, but Agnes Pratchett also — along with my daughter."

"Never!" Mrs. Quaver declared, though Will and I exchanged meaningful glances. I believe that we were beginning to understand.

"How I searched for them. I hired detectives, such as those you read of in *Sherlock Holmes*, but just when I thought that I had found her, the woman slipped away again. It seemed that she had the modus operandi of setting up in a cheap tenement, then moving on in a matter of weeks. She was always on the move and, as far as I could learn, always taking a train from one town to another. And then, after I had searched for a good two years, the trail ran cold. My detectives refused to take my brief, declaring it a 'waste of time,' even telling me that Pratchett must have emigrated, taking my darling with her. But I never gave up hope, nor did I stop searching. Since that time I have looked in every paper for the name of Agnes Pratchett, and when I could I would search railway stations, jostling among the crowds for a glimpse of her — or the face of my little one. Until the trial I had no joy, and then—"

"That is where I saw you," I burst out. "I saw you at the trial. And my name is Sarah. And I was brought up by Agnes Pratchett. Tell me, what was your little girl's name?"

"I called her Sarah Bronte Islington."

"And there is no evidence? No papers?" Will asked, almost as excited as myself.

"I know of something that is more certain than papers," Lady Islington said, reaching down to stroke my hair again. "My Sarah had a birthmark on the nape of her neck. If I could ..." Here she leant towards me, and I willingly threw my hair forwards so that the back of my neck was revealed.

"Did the birthmark have a special shape?" I muttered, my head down.

"Yes, it looked like the tiniest star. Here, Mrs. Quaver, come and see. I am looking at it now."

I felt the touch of her soft leather glove and a shiver ran down my spine. Then her hand shifted and, cupping my chin, she raised my head.

"I believe that you are my daughter," she said, "Sarah Bronte Islington," and tears welled in her eyes.

But I could only whisper, "Mama," and thank those far-off midnight stars that my dazzling dreams of the future were shining through at last.

Epilogue

In the years that followed, "Maman," as she chose to be called, saw to my education and taught me all her skills in drawing and watercolor. As she had before me, I devoted my life to my art and toured the globe with her, filling folio after folio with botanical sketches and paintings of the wonders that we saw.

Nor did I forget dear Will during all these travels. From time to time he journeyed with us, adding the pleasure of his company to our happiness, until such time as he asked Maman for my hand in marriage. To this she readily assented.

Now, as I write, I hear the voices of my own little ones, and it is that sweet sound which will, I trust, drive away those bitter memories of my life with Mama so many years ago.